HELP! I'm Trapped in My Teacher's Body

Other books by Todd Strasser:

The Diving Bell

Friends Till the End

The Accident

Home Alone™ (novelization)

Home Alone 2™ (novelization)

The Mall from Outer Space

Beyond the Reef

The Complete Computer Popularity Program

HELP! I'm Trapped in My Teacher's Body

TODD STRASSER

AN
APPLE
PAPERBACK

SCHOLASTIC INC.
New York Toronto London Auckland Sydney

No part of this publication may be reproduced in whole or in part, or stored in a retrieval system, or transmitted in any form or by any means, electronic, mechanical, photocopying, recording, or otherwise, without written permission of the publisher. For information regarding permission, write to Scholastic Inc., 730 Broadway, New York, NY 10003.

ISBN 0-590-47737-4

Copyright © 1993 by Todd Strasser. All rights reserved. Published by Scholastic Inc. APPLE PAPERBACKS® is a registered trademark of Scholastic Inc.

12 11 10 9 8 7 6 5   6 7 8/9

Printed in the U.S.A.   40

First Scholastic printing, September 1993

To Lia, with all my love

HELP! I'm Trapped in My Teacher's Body

1

"Gentlemen, prepare your spitballs," Josh whispered. We were in Mr. Dorksen's science class. His real name is Dirksen, but no one called him that.

Josh, Andy Kent, and I tore off pieces of notebook paper and slipped them into our mouths. Mr. Dorksen was standing by the blackboard talking about cow stomachs.

"When cows eat, they moisten their food with saliva," Mr. Dorksen said.

Josh turned and winked at Andy and me as we moistened our spitballs with saliva. In the next row, Amanda Gluck started to cough and raised her hand.

Mr. Dorksen stared at her through thick glasses that made his eyes look tiny. "Yes, Amanda?"

"Can I get some water?"

"You know the rules, Amanda," Mr. Dorksen said. "No water during class."

Amanda coughed again. Like Mr. Dorksen,

Amanda wore glasses. Each time she coughed, her glasses slid down her nose. "But I really need it."

"The answer is no." Mr. Dorksen turned back to the blackboard and pointed at a large drawing of a cow and its stomachs.

"Now where was I?" he said. "Oh, yes. When a cow eats grass, the grass goes down the esophagus and into the first stomach. Does anyone know what the first stomach is called?"

It was a little hard to hear Mr. Dorksen because Amanda was still hacking away. Josh turned to Andy and me again.

"Gentlemen, load your spitballs," he whispered.

"Josh?" Mr. Dorksen said. "Are you volunteering an answer?"

Josh spun around in his seat. He's the biggest kid in class and has reddish hair and freckles. "I'm sorry, Mr. Dork . . . er, I mean, Dirksen. What did you say?"

The class tittered. Except for Amanda Gluck, who was coughing too much to titter. She'd given up on trying to keep her glasses straight. Now they just hung crookedly on the tip of her nose and threatened to fall off.

Mr. Dorksen ran his skinny hand over his shiny bald head and looked annoyed. "I asked if you knew what a cow's first stomach is called?"

"What it's called?"

"Yes, Josh," Mr. Dorksen said. "The name of the first stomach."

"Uh, how about Ralph?"

The class cracked up. Mr. Dorksen's tiny eyes narrowed with anger. His forehead wrinkled. His beard bristled.

"Well, if you don't like Ralph," Josh said, "how about Archibald?"

The class was really in hysterics now.

"Stop it!" Mr. Dorksen shouted at all of us. "Stop it right now, or I'll send all of you to the principal's office!"

The class quieted down. Mr. Dorksen took a handkerchief out of his pocket and patted his forehead with it. Then he glared at us.

"At home, I am working on an experiment designed to electronically transfer learning from one animal to another," he told us. "I hope that someday it will be used on humans, thus replacing the need for teachers and school."

"Way to go!" Andy shouted with a big grin that showed off his braces. The rest of the class started to cheer.

"No more school! No more school!"

"Shut up!" Mr. Dorksen shouted.

The class got quiet again.

"Unfortunately, the experiment is still in the developmental stage," Mr. Dorksen said. "So in the meantime, we are stuck with each other. Believe me, I am just as unhappy about it as you are. But if you could somehow learn to behave, it would make this year much easier for all of us."

On the other side of the room, Julia Saks raised her hand. Julia had blonde hair, big brown eyes, a perfect nose, and pretty eyebrows. She knew she was the prettiest girl in class. She also had a reputation for saying exactly what was on her mind. "Maybe this class would be more fun if you didn't just stand up there and lecture us all the time. After all, this *is* science. Maybe we should do some experiments or something."

Mr. Dorksen took off his glasses and breathed on them. He squinted at us while he rubbed the glasses with his handkerchief.

"You know, Julia," he replied, "I really wish that just for once one of you students could be the teacher and I could be the student. I'd love to see how you'd handle a classroom filled with such ill-mannered, ill-behaved sixth-graders as yourselves. The thought of letting you do an experiment is preposterous."

He pointed to a long row of glass cabinets along one wall. Inside we could see jars filled with different-colored chemicals.

"Do you realize that most of those chemicals are poisonous?" Mr. Dorksen asked. "Some are even explosive. How could I possibly allow you to do an experiment? If you didn't poison yourselves, you would probably blow us all up."

About once a week Mr. Dorksen told us that we were the worst sixth-grade class he'd ever taught, and why he couldn't trust us to do anything except sit in our seats.

Meanwhile, Josh, Andy, and I loaded our soggy spitballs into hollowed-out Bic pens. Mr. Dorksen looked up at the clock.

"The class is almost over," he said. "As usual, you have wasted a great deal of time. Therefore, instead of reading one chapter tonight, you will read two."

The class groaned while Mr. Dorksen wrote the homework assignment on the blackboard. Josh turned to Andy and me.

"Ready . . . ," he whispered, "aim . . . *fire!*"

Three spitballs shot through the air. Two hit the blackboard and one hit Mr. Dorksen on the back of the hand.

"*What the . . . ?*" Mr. Dorksen spun around and squinted at us, looking for the culprits. Josh and Andy quickly hid their spitball shooters in their desks. I tried to hide mine, but it slipped out of my hand and clattered onto the floor.

"Jake Sherman." Mr. Dorksen glared angrily at me and wiped the spitball off his hand. "You will remain after class."

2

I sat at my desk while Mr. Dorksen waited for the class to leave. Not that I was scared or anything. The worst Mr. Dorksen could do was send me to Principal Blanco's office or give me detention. I had plenty of experience at both and didn't particularly care.

Mr. Dorksen was the worst teacher I'd ever had. He wouldn't let anyone get a drink of water or go to the bathroom during class, and he gave three times as much homework as any other teacher.

And, like Julia Saks said, he was boring. He just stood in the front of the class every day and lectured us. And every Friday he gave us a super-hard quiz. We'd been in school for a month and a half, and Andy hadn't passed one yet.

The door closed as the last student went out. I wondered what kind of punishment Mr. Dorksen was planning for me. One thing Mr. Dorksen had a lot of experience at was punishing kids.

"Come up here, Jake," he said.

I went up to his desk. I wasn't as big as Josh, but I wasn't small either. Mr. Dorksen didn't scare me. He was thin and wore baggy brown jackets, brown pants, and brown shoes. His skin was so pale you could see the blue veins in the backs of his hands.

Once again he took off his thick glasses and exhaled on them and then rubbed them with his handkerchief.

"You know, Jake, I had your sister, Jessica, when she was in sixth grade," he said. "I still see her in homeroom every day. It's hard to believe that the two of you come from the same family."

"A lot of people say that."

"Do they?" Mr. Dorksen pretended to be surprised. "Why do you think that is?"

"Simple," I said. "Jessica is a total brain, superior athlete, and all around extraterrestrial. I, on the other hand, am a mere human being."

For just one second Mr. Dorksen smirked. Then he said, "You know, I could send you to Principal Blanco's office for shooting spitballs. Or I could give you a week's worth of detention. But I'm not going to do either. Would you like to know why?"

I shook my head.

"Because I don't think you really care, Jake. In fact, you don't seem to care about anything except disrupting my class. So, instead, I've come up with a different way for you to make up for your

7

misbehavior. You see that box?" Mr. Dorksen pointed toward the corner of the room where a large cardboard box sat on the floor. The box was covered with red FRAGILE stickers.

I nodded.

"You are going to carry that home for me after school today."

That didn't seem like such a big deal to me. "What's in it?"

"A magnetic resonance high-frequency oscilloscope," Mr. Dorksen said. "And with it I will be able to complete my learning transfer experiment. Unfortunately, it is quite heavy and I have a bad back."

"Why don't you just put it in your car?" I asked.

"Because my car is in the shop, being repaired," Mr. Dorksen said. "Another teacher has been giving me a ride to school each morning."

"Then why don't you call a cab or ask that teacher to drive you home?"

"Because I want *you* to carry it," Mr. Dorksen said. "Or, if you would prefer, your punishment can be copying by hand the first five pages of the unabridged dictionary."

"Is that the big one with the tiny print?" I asked.

"That's correct."

"I'll carry the box."

"I thought so," Mr. Dorksen said with a smile.

"And while we walk home, we will have a talk about why you feel it is so important to disrupt my class constantly."

I can't say I was looking forward to it.

After Mr. Dorksen's class, I had lunch. I go to the Burt Itchupt Middle School (we call it Burp It Up). Burp It Up is pretty new. They built it about five years ago because Jeffersonville, the town I live in, was growing so fast. It used to be all farms around here, but now it's mostly houses owned by people who drive to the city to work.

Josh and Andy were waiting for me at our regular table in the cafeteria. Andy is about my height, but a lot thinner. He parts his black hair in the middle and bites his nails a lot.

"So what'd Dorkhead do?" he asked as he munched on some French fries. A scuffed football lay on the table beside him.

"Not much. I just have to carry a box home for him after school."

"That's all?" Josh asked through a mouthful of pizza. "Sounds like you got off easy."

"He said we're gonna talk about why I mess around so much in his class," I said.

"What a drag," Andy said. "You're not mad that you got caught and we didn't, are you?"

I shook my head. I knew it wasn't their fault. I took a bite out of the peanut butter and jelly

9

sandwich I'd brought from home. Josh took another bite of the pizza he'd just bought. His cheeks bulged.

"So you guys looking forward to the camping trip?" I asked.

"It's gonna be so cool," Josh said. "Just the three of us out in the woods in your parents' cabin with all the soda and junk food we can eat."

"You're sure your parents aren't gonna change their minds?" Andy asked, picking some gunk out of his braces.

"Pretty sure," I said. "My father said he'll drive us up there Friday night and come get us Sunday afternoon. He just made me promise I wouldn't wreck the place."

"Hey, Jake," Josh said, staring past me. "Maybe you should ask Ms. Rogers if she wants to come."

I turned around. Ms. Rogers was walking toward us. She's a new young social studies teacher who has sixth-grade lunch duty. Her hair is wavy and black, and her eyes are big and blue. Her cheeks are rosy, but it isn't from makeup. Unlike my other teachers, she's really nice and easy to talk to.

"Forget it," Andy said, grinning and nudging me with his elbow. "If Ms. Rogers came, Jake wouldn't want us around."

"Get off it, phlegmwad." I pushed him away.

Josh leaned across the table toward me. "Come

on, Jake. Everyone knows you have a crush on her."

"Do not." I stared down at my half-eaten peanut butter and jelly sandwich.

"Then how come you turn red every time we talk about her?" Andy asked.

"Do not," I said.

"Do not. Do not," Josh mimicked me.

"Look out," Andy whispered. "Here she comes!"

"Bet you a nickel she rubs Jake's head and asks how her favorite troublemaker is," Josh whispered back.

"Forget it."

"Give you three to one odds," Josh whispered.

"*Five* to one," Andy said.

"Deal."

Ms. Rogers stopped by our table. She was wearing red slacks and a big blue sweater with shiny stars sewn onto it. It seemed like she always wore slacks and sweaters.

"How's my favorite troublemaker?" She rubbed my head.

"Way to go." Andy groaned, reached into his pocket for a nickel, and flipped it to Josh.

"Aren't you a little young to be making money bets?" Ms. Rogers asked with a knowing smile.

Josh, Andy, and I glanced at each other. We probably would have had some wisecrack for any other teacher.

"Hey, Ms. Rogers," Andy said. "You don't really think we're bad guys, do you? I mean, not like hoods or anything."

"No, you're not hoods," Ms. Rogers said. "You're just good kids who act up. You'll get it out of your systems someday."

"What'll have to happen for us to get it out of our systems?" Andy asked.

"Oh, I guess you'll just have to see things from the other side."

Josh, Andy, and I frowned at each other.

"What do you mean, from the other side?" I asked.

Ms. Rogers put her hand on my shoulder. She did that sometimes. "You'll know when it happens, Jake."

3

We finished lunch. Josh picked up the football. "Who's up for catch?" he asked.

"I am," I said.

"Not me," said Andy. "I'm gonna fly my kite."

"Not that again," Josh groaned. "You've been trying to fly that stupid kite for weeks."

"I'm sure it's gonna fly this time," Andy insisted. He'd made the kite in shop class. He always tried to fly it at lunch, but so far it had never gotten off the ground.

Andy went to get his kite, and Josh and I went out to the playground. The playground at Burp It Up Middle School is huge and covered with asphalt. You can easily have a couple of basketball games, a football game, and a baseball game all going at the same time without worrying about people banging into each other.

It had gotten really cloudy since that morning. Windy, too. Josh and I started to throw the football around.

"Let's see who can throw it the farthest," Josh said. He stayed at one end of the playground while I went down to the other end. We started to throw the football back and forth. Each time one of us caught it, we'd back up a little more.

Josh heaved the ball toward me. I was just about to catch it when someone ran in front of me and grabbed it first.

"Hey!" I shouted. The person turned around, and I saw that it was my sister, Jessica. She was a couple of inches taller than me and had long brown hair that was always braided down her back. She had a few freckles on her nose, but not nearly as many as Josh.

"Got a problem?" she asked, brushing her brown bangs out of her eyes.

"Yeah, *you*."

Jessica waved Josh back.

"You'll never be able to throw it *that* far," I said.

"Bet?"

"The dinner dishes," I said.

"Deal." Jessica pulled her arm back and let go a perfect spiral. Josh actually had to back up another few feet to catch it. Jessica grinned at me. "Double or nothing?"

"No fair," I said. "The wind carried it."

"Too bad. A bet's a bet."

She could make me so mad. "Why do you always

have to interfere with my life?" I yelled. "How come you always have to show how much better you are? What are you doing out here anyway? This isn't eighth-grade lunch."

"I have to eat this period because there's a special student government meeting during fifth period lunch," Jessica said.

Not only was my sister a better student and athlete than me, but she was president of the student body as well.

"You make me sick," I said.

"From you that's a compliment," Jessica said and walked away.

Josh came back with the football. "Your sister has some arm."

"The wind helped," I muttered.

"Hey, guys!"

Josh and I turned around and saw Andy coming toward us carrying his red kite. It was shaped like a big V.

"You'll never get that thing into the air," Josh said.

"You're wrong," Andy said. "I made some modifications."

"Like what?" Josh asked. "You added an engine?"

"Just watch," Andy said.

He went down to the end of the playground and ran toward us. The wind caught the kite almost immediately, and it shot straight up into the sky.

"See, it really works!" Andy cried, letting the string out as he ran.

But suddenly the kite turned and headed straight down.

At us!

"Look out!" Josh shouted.

We all dove out of the way.

Crash! A second later, the kite crashed into the playground just a few feet from Josh. Andy jumped up and ran over to it. The nose was completely crushed, and one wing had snapped in two.

"See!" he yelled gleefully. "It flew!"

"Until it crashed," I said. "You built the world's first kamikaze kite!"

"It nearly killed me!" Josh screamed as he got up and brushed off his jeans.

"A small price to pay," Andy said with a smile.

When school was over, I went back to Mr. Dorksen's room. He had put on a coat and a brown wool cap even though it wasn't that cold out.

"Ready, Jake?" he said.

"Yeah." I bent down and picked up the box. It was pretty heavy, and I had a hard time getting a grip on it.

"Careful," Mr. Dorksen said. "That's a very expensive piece of equipment."

"You're gonna make me carry this *all* the way to your house?" I asked, grimacing.

"You can stop for a rest now and then," Mr. Dorksen replied.

What a guy, huh?

We got outside and started walking along the sidewalk. It was really windy now, and the sky was filled with heavy gray clouds.

"Looks like a storm is coming," Mr. Dorksen said. "We better hurry."

"You could always call a cab," I reminded him.

Instead of answering, Mr. Dorksen just started to walk faster.

"So tell me, Jake," he said, "have you ever wondered why you're so disruptive?"

"I don't know," I said, trying to keep a grip on the box.

"Maybe it has something to do with your sister."

"Let me guess," I said. "She's such a brain and good athlete that I know I can't compete so I rebel?"

"I see you've heard that before."

"About six thousand times."

We stopped at a corner and waited for the light to change; then we crossed the street. Trees were shaking and bending. The wind was blowing so hard it was tearing the leaves off the branches. I didn't know where Mr. Dorksen lived, but I hoped it wasn't too far away.

"Let me put it to you differently," Mr. Dorksen said. "Is there any way that I could get you to be less disruptive in my class?"

17

"Uh, if I answer truthfully, will I get into trouble?"

"No, Jake."

"Well, remember what Julia Saks said about class being so boring?" I asked. "You could try making it interesting."

Mr. Dorksen didn't answer right away. We walked down the block and then crossed another street. The wind felt damp, like it was going to rain any second.

"Tell me," Mr. Dorksen finally said, "are all your other classes that much more interesting than mine?"

"No."

"Then why does *my* class have to be interesting?" Mr. Dorksen asked.

"Well, you wouldn't expect a dumb subject like math or social studies to be interesting," I said. "But science could be fun. I mean, we could do experiments, like make bombs or something."

"Bombs?" Mr. Dorksen winced.

"Sure. Why not?"

Mr. Dorksen didn't answer. He just sighed, shook his head, and kept walking.

It took a while to get to Mr. Dorksen's house. By then my arms were really killing me from lugging the box. The wind had gotten even stronger, blowing leaves and loose newspapers around. Mr. Dorksen lived in a small brown house in a community about a mile from school. Tall power line towers ran through the field behind the house. Just as we got to the driveway, monster raindrops started to splash down around us. I could hear thunder in the distance.

"Hurry," Mr. Dorksen said, jogging up his driveway. Instead of going into the house, he pulled open the garage door and we went inside.

Mr. Dorksen flicked on the lights.

"Oh, wow," I said as I put the box down. The inside of Mr. Dorksen's garage looked like a science lab crammed with all kinds of electronic gear.

"This is my experiment," Mr. Dorksen said proudly.

"You said you wanted to do something to animals," I said, looking around.

"I'm surprised you paid that much attention," Mr. Dorksen replied as he started to open the box. "Actually, I'm experimenting with electronic transference of intelligence. The theory being that you can transfer intelligence from one creature to another using electromagnetic waves."

Outside, it had started to pour. The rain hammered the roof, and the thunder was growing louder.

"Looks like you're going to be stuck here for a while, Jake," Mr. Dorksen said. "Perhaps you'd like to help me install the magnetic resonating high-frequency oscilloscope."

"Will I get extra credit?"

19

Mr. Dorksen rolled his eyes. "Sure, Jake."

The experiment took up most of the garage, but basically there were two cages with a whole bunch of wires and computer consoles in between them. Mr. Dorksen showed me where to plug the cables from the oscilloscope into panels behind the cages.

Outside, thunder crashed and the sky was lit by lightning. Mr. Dorksen stared out the open garage door at the pouring rain.

"Sounds like the storm is heading right toward us," he said.

"What's this for?" I held up a spool of super-thin wire.

"That's ultra-thin, super-flexible high-voltage wire," Mr. Dorksen said. "I'm using it for the experiment. Otherwise I'd be mired in one huge tangle of wires."

I kept plugging things in. "This is like setting up a super-CD system."

"Well, I wouldn't know about that," Mr. Dorksen replied. "Basically, I will put a trained animal in cage A. That's the cage you're working on. And an untrained animal of the same species in cage B. Which is the cage I'm working on. If my calculations are correct, the result will be two trained animals."

"And you really think you could use this on people?"

"Yes," Mr. Dorksen said. "The day may soon come when the concept of student and teacher will be obsolete. All knowledge will be acquired electronically."

"Cool," I said.

"Believe me," Mr. Dorksen said, "I'll be just as thrilled as you."

There was another loud clap of thunder, followed by a sudden flash of lightning. Mr. Dorksen looked a little worried.

"You know, Jake," he said nervously, "maybe we should stop working on this for a moment."

"Why?"

"Well, I know it's rather unlikely," he said, "but if by any chance lightning were to — "

Ka-Boom! Suddenly, there was a blinding flash of lightning right over us, followed by a huge crash of thunder. The whole garage shook, and I felt a strong tingling sensation all over.

Then everything went black.

4

When I opened my eyes, I was lying on the cool, concrete floor of the garage. Outside, the rain had stopped, and all I heard was the *split-splat* of water dripping off the roof. Everything in the garage looked kind of fuzzy. I pushed myself to my feet and stood up. Everything looked different. Not just fuzzy, but different.

A kid was walking toward me. He looked fuzzy, too. But I could see that he had brown hair like mine. Even stranger, he was wearing a pair of jeans and a green and white long-sleeved polo shirt just like the shirt I wore that day.

He stopped a few feet away, and we just stared at each other. Even though he was fuzzy, he looked really familiar.

"Incredible," he gasped.

"What?" I said. That was weird. My voice had changed.

"Don't you realize what's happened?"

"No, and who are you anyway?" I asked. I kept trying to squint, but I just couldn't see him clearly.

He bent down, picked something up off the floor, and handed it to me. Glasses.

"Put them on."

"Why?" I asked. "I don't wear glasses."

"You do now."

I put them on. Everything suddenly came into focus. Including the kid. I felt goose bumps run down my arms and legs, and it was hard to breathe. The kid looked exactly like me!

I pinched myself. It hurt. I was pretty sure I wasn't dreaming.

"What is this?" I gasped.

"The experiment," the kid said.

"What about it?"

"I'm Mr. Dirksen," said the kid.

"You turned yourself into me?" I asked, totally amazed.

"Yes."

"Oh, wow! This is totally bizarre!"

"More so than you'd think," said Mr. Dirksen, who now looked exactly like me.

"What do you mean?"

"Put your hand on your head."

I did it. The top of my head felt smooth and hairless.

"Touch your chin," he said.

23

My chin was covered with hair.

"Look at yourself."

I was wearing a brown jacket, brown pants, and brown leather shoes. I looked down at my hands. My fingers were long and bony, and I could see blue veins through the skin.

"Ohmygod!" I cried.

Mr. Dirksen . . . I mean, me . . . I mean, Mr. Dirksen nodded. "We've switched."

I'd become Mr. Dorksen! Talk about a fate worse than death!

"You've got to switch us back!" I cried.

"I don't know if I can," Mr. Dirksen said. "It's not that easy."

"What do you mean?" I gasped. "You switched us. Of course you can switch us back."

"I'm afraid not," he said. "You see, my house must have been struck by lightning. The bars of the cages must have spread the force around us. It had to take an extraordinary amount of electricity to switch us completely. It's practically impossible to generate that kind of electricity by normal means."

"But you don't understand," I said. "I can't be you. Everyone will hate me! This is the worst thing that ever happened!"

Mr. Dorksen, I mean, I stared back at me and didn't say a word. He looked at his, I mean, my hands and feet. Then he jumped up and down.

Then he bent backwards and forwards at the waist.

"My back hasn't felt this good in years," he said.

"That's because it's not your back!" I shouted. "It's *my* back! And I want it back."

"Do you?" A smirk grew on my . . . I mean, Mr. Dorksen's face.

"Look," I said. "I don't know what you think is so funny, but I have to go home and have dinner. I can't go home looking like you. My parents will have a fit."

"I imagine they would," he said with a devilish look. He slid his hand into his jeans pocket.

"Hey!" I shouted. "Get your hand out of my pocket!"

Mr. Dirksen found my wallet and took out a small white card. "Fake ID?"

"We had them made up as a joke," I said. "I mean, nobody would ever believe I was over twenty-one."

"They will now," Mr. Dirksen said. He read the card. "Jake Sherman, twenty-six Magnolia Drive. I know where that is."

"So?"

"Can't be late for dinner, Mr. *Dork*sen." He winked at me and jogged out of the garage.

"Hey!" I gasped. "Where are you going?"

"To my house," he shouted back.

"But *this* is your house," I said.

"Not anymore!"

It wasn't easy to run in those stupid brown leather shoes. And I couldn't believe how out of breath I got, or how much my back hurt. Soon Mr. Dirksen, in my body, was just a speck a couple of blocks ahead of me. I ran about twenty yards at a time, but then I had to slow to a walk and gasp for air. Mr. Dirksen's dumb heart was beating so hard I was afraid I might have a heart attack. And his knees hurt, too.

By the time I got to my neighborhood, Mr. Dirksen, in my body, was so far ahead that I couldn't see him. Mr. Dirksen's knees had started to really ache, and his back hurt so much I could hardly stand up straight.

What a crummy body! I thought.

It was starting to get dark by the time I got to Magnolia Drive. As I hobbled down the sidewalk past my neighbors' houses, I could see some of them sitting with their families in their kitchens and dining rooms eating dinner. That's what I was supposed to be doing. Not limping around in my science teacher's stupid body.

Finally I got to my house and went up the walk. I tried the front door but it was locked. I reached into my pocket for my key, but instead found a key ring with a dozen keys on it. *Mr. Dorksen's keys!*

I rang the doorbell.

Inside, I heard my mother say, "I wonder who that could be?"

Then I heard my father say, "Jessica, get the door."

Chair legs scraped on the floor, and footsteps approached the door. A second later it swung open. Jessica stared at me and frowned while I stared past her into the dining room. I couldn't believe it! Mr. Dorksen, in *my* body, was sitting in *my* chair, eating *my dinner*!

"Mr. Dirksen? What are you doing here?" Jessica asked.

"I'm not Mr. Dirksen," I said, stepping into the house. "I'm Jake, your brother."

As I walked toward the dining room table, I watched my mother and my father give each other nervous looks. Jake, I mean, Mr. Dirksen just stared down at his pot roast and mashed potatoes.

"What seems to be the problem, Mr. Dirksen?" my father asked.

"The problem is that I'm not Mr. Dirksen," I said. "I'm your son, Jake. Tell them, Mr. Dirksen."

My parents stared at Mr. Dirksen, in *my* body.

"Mom, Dad, I don't know what he's talking about," Mr. Dirksen said.

"It does sound rather extraordinary," my father said staring back at me.

So I told them how it happened.

"You and Jake accidently switched bodies when lightning hit your house?" my mother asked, clearly bewildered.

"Not me and Jake," I said. "I *am* Jake. And lightning hit *his* house." Again I pointed at that imposter in my body.

My father frowned. "Lightning didn't hit our house."

"No, it hit *his* house!"

"But this is Jake's house," my mother said.

"Are you guys deaf?" I asked. "I told you we switched bodies."

"Should I call the police?" Jessica asked, standing near the kitchen doorway.

"Would you stay out of this!" I yelled at her.

"Mr. Dirksen!" my mother gasped.

"I would appreciate it if you did not speak to my daughter that way," my father said, getting out of his chair. My father is about five inches taller than Mr. Dirksen and weighs about forty pounds more. He works out at the gym four days a week. He was still wearing his tie from work, but his sleeves were rolled up. I knew he could squash me like a bug if he wanted to.

I stared at Mr. Dirksen in my body. "You can't get away with this, Mr. Dirksen. You've got to tell them the truth."

"Why does he keep calling me Mr. Dirksen?" Jake, I mean, Mr. Dirksen asked.

"You liar!" I gasped.

My father stepped closer to me. "I think it's time you went home, Mr. Dirksen. Or I really will call the police."

I stared at my father, then at my mother and sister. They didn't believe me! They actually thought that bogus dweeb sitting in my chair was me!

"You have to listen to me Dad," I pleaded. "That's not me sitting in that chair. I know it looks just like me, but it isn't."

"Go home, Mr. Dirksen," my father said firmly. "And please don't come back. I'd hate to have to tell the school about this incident."

"But you don't understand!" I gasped.

"I understand just fine," my father said. "Now please go."

I glared at Mr. Dirksen in my body. "I'll get you for this!"

"Go, Mr. Dirksen!" my father said firmly. "I will not allow you to come into this house and threaten my son."

It was no use. I backed toward the door and glanced at Jessica one last time. Suddenly I had an idea.

"Nice throw today," I said. "Too bad the wind carried it."

Jessica frowned.

"What did he mean by that?" my father asked.

Jessica's eyes darted back and forth from me to my father. "Uh, nothing."

"Why don't you ask Jake what I meant," I said.

My father frowned. "For the last time, Mr. Dirksen, either leave this house or I will call the police."

The next thing I knew, I was thrown out of my own house.

5

I was totally bummed out. Imagine being trapped in your teacher's body and no one believes you. I thought about going to Andy's or Josh's house, but why would they believe me?

Finally, I walked back to Mr. Dirksen's house. It was really dark, and there were no lights on inside. My back was killing me and my knees ached. I let myself in the front door with his key. It was dark inside and I flicked on a light.

Everything in Mr. Dirksen's house was brown. The carpet, the furniture, the walls, even the refrigerator and stove! All the furniture looked like it had been picked up in a secondhand store.

Everything was incredibly neat and organized. The books on the bookshelves were in neat rows. The magazines on the coffee table were arranged from biggest to smallest. All the window shades were pulled the same length.

I tried the TV. The picture was full of static. I

changed the channels. What a bummer! Mr. Dirk-sen didn't even have cable! I looked around for a CD player, but all Mr. Dirksen had was a stereo. With records!

Next I went into the kitchen and looked in the refrigerator. All there was were some eggs, half a bag of Wonder bread, a package of American cheese slices, and some sour-smelling milk.

I slammed the refrigerator door shut. It was hopeless! I hated being Mr. Dirksen. I hated his body and I hated his house. I slumped down at the kitchen table, feeling like I was going to cry. Here I was, stuck in my teacher's crummy body, stuck in his crummy home, with no food and no cable. Meanwhile, someone else was living in my house, pretending to be me. Even my parents believed him!

I sniffed and felt a tear run out of Mr. Dirksen's eye. I tried to wipe it away, but Mr. Dirksen's stupid glasses got in the way.

Why me? I wondered. *What have I ever done to deserve this?*

Then I remembered what Ms. Rogers said at lunch. *"You'll just have to see things from the other side . . ."*

Was this my punishment for always getting into trouble? I stared up at the soundproof tiles on Mr. Dirksen's kitchen ceiling.

"Oh, please," I whispered. "Please let me be

Jake again. I promise I'll be super good for the rest of my life."

I waited, but nothing happened.

After a while, Mr. Dirksen's stomach started to growl. I sat up and looked around at the kitchen, wondering what I'd eat. Then I realized that I was sitting on something hard and square. I reached into the back pocket of Mr. Dirksen's pants. His wallet!

I took it out. Inside was sixty-five dollars in cash and a MasterCard. I couldn't help smiling a little. Every cloud had a silver lining. At least I wasn't going to go hungry.

I ordered pizza and soda from Domino's and watched fuzzy TV until it was late. Finally I felt tired enough to go to sleep. I went into the bathroom and looked at myself in the mirror. Mr. Dirksen's beady little eyes stared back at me through his glasses. I almost looked older than my own father!

My mouth felt filmy, but the idea of brushing my teeth with Mr. Dirksen's toothbrush made me ill, so I used my finger instead. Then I yawned, but the thought of sleeping in Mr. Dirksen's bed was so repulsive that I got a sheet and blanket out of the linen closet and made a bed on the couch. Then I went around locking the doors and turning off all the lights except the one next to the couch.

Finally I took off Mr. Dirksen's dumb clothes

and got into bed. I had to lie on my side with my legs tucked up. That was the only position in which Mr. Dirksen's dumb back didn't hurt. Before I turned off the light, I looked around Mr. Dirksen's brown living room for one last time. What a miserable life the guy must have had. Could that be why he was so mean?

6

A bell was ringing. I opened my eyes and looked around. For a second I didn't know where I was. Then it all came back. I was trapped in Mr. Dirksen's body.

Briiinggg! The bell rang again.

"Just a minute!" I said, sitting up. My back was stiff. My mouth felt cottony, and my breath smelled weird. But I didn't care. I was sure Mr. Dirksen had come to his senses and told my parents the truth. They'd come to rescue me! I quickly pulled on his pants. Then I stood up and headed for the door. Suddenly I realized I couldn't see anything.

Briiinnnnggg! The bell rang insistently.

"Just one more second!" I stumbled back to the couch and felt around for his glasses. Boy, I couldn't wait to get my own body back. Finally I found the glasses and put them on. A second later I pulled open the door.

Only my parents weren't standing outside. Ms. Rogers was!

"Ms. Rogers!" I stammered.

"Phil!" Ms. Roger's jaw dropped and her big blue eyes went wide. Today she was wearing a light blue sweater with flowers, and she'd put her hair up.

"Who's Phil?" I asked. I still couldn't believe Ms. Rogers was standing there. I began to get that nervous feeling I felt whenever she was around.

Ms. Rogers scowled at me. "Are you feeling all right, Phil?"

"Uh . . ." It suddenly occurred to me that Phil must have been Mr. Dirksen's first name. "What are you doing here?"

"You haven't called in sick, have you?" Ms. Rogers asked.

"Uh, no . . ."

"Well, I'm here to give you a ride because your car is in the shop," Ms. Rogers said. "Now, you better get dressed or you'll be late. Have you had breakfast?"

"Er . . . no."

"All right," Ms. Rogers said, pushing up the sleeves of her sweater. "You get dressed, and I'll make you some breakfast."

The next thing I knew, Ms. Rogers went past me and into the kitchen. She and Mr. Dirksen must have been friends or something. I heard the refrigerator open and close.

"You really don't have to make me breakfast," I said.

"Oh, come on, Phil. How on earth do you expect to teach a whole morning of classes on an empty stomach?"

Teach classes? Me? Uh-oh . . . Now I was really in trouble. How could *I* teach?

I wondered if I should try telling her the truth. I'd always thought Ms. Rogers was the nicest and most understanding teacher I knew, but I doubted she'd believe that I was now trapped in Mr. Dirksen's body.

Ms. Rogers stuck her head out of the kitchen and gave me a funny look. "You better get dressed, Phil. We don't have much time."

I went into Mr. Dirksen's bedroom and opened his closet. Every shirt and pair of pants was hanging in a perfect line. Mr. Dirksen didn't have a lot of clothes, but I found a pair of jeans, a plain white shirt, and a pair of tennis shoes. On the floor was an old baseball mitt with a scratched, dirty ball in it. It made me wonder if Mr. Dirksen had once played ball.

There wasn't time to dwell on it. Still feeling nervous, I went into the bathroom and looked in the mirror. Mr. Dirksen stared back at me through those thick glasses.

Wait a minute, I thought. *Ms. Rogers doesn't know it's you. She thinks it's Mr. Dirksen!*

Suddenly I didn't feel so nervous. So what if I did or said anything dumb? She'd think it was Mr. Dirksen.

Ms. Rogers called from the kitchen. "Phil, your breakfast is ready."

I went into the kitchen. Ms. Rogers had placed a plate of steaming eggs and toast on the kitchen table. She looked surprised.

"Is that what you're wearing to school today?" she asked.

"Sure. Why not?"

"Oh, I don't know," she said. "I guess it's just not like you. But I have to admit, you look good in jeans."

"Well, thanks," I said, sitting down. "And may I say that you look very pretty with your hair like that. And that's a very nice sweater."

Ms. Rogers blushed. "That's the first time you've ever said anything like that to me, Phil."

"That doesn't mean I haven't been thinking it," I said with a wink. Flirting with Ms. Rogers was fun. I couldn't wait to tell Andy and Josh about this!

The tea kettle whistled, and Ms. Rogers poured the steaming water into a cup. Except she spilled some of it.

"Oh, dear!" she cried.

"Are you okay?" I started to get up.

"Oh, yes, don't get up." She mopped up the spilled water with a paper towel. I could see she was sort of flustered. She finished making her tea and sat down at the table with me while I gulped down some eggs and toast.

"Delicious!" I said. "You ought to make breakfast for me more often."

Ms. Rogers laughed nervously. "My, Phil, you're certainly in rare form this morning!"

"You could say I feel like a new me, Ms. Rogers," I said.

Ms. Rogers suddenly frowned. "Why do you keep calling me that, Phil?"

"Calling you what?" I asked.

"Ms. Rogers. You know my first name."

"Huh? Oh, uh, you see . . ." She'd really caught me there.

"I know you're feeling different this morning," Ms. Rogers said, "but you can still call me Kim."

"Kim," I repeated.

Ms. Rogers glanced up at the kitchen clock. "Oh, my gosh!" she gasped. "We're going to be late! We'd better go!"

I had time to stuff one last bite of toast in my mouth before we hurried out and got into Ms. Rogers's car. The next thing I knew, I was on my way to school.

To be a teacher for the first time in my life.

7

First period was homeroom, and the first person to arrive in homeroom was Jessica. She gave me a funny look as she sat down at her desk.

"Did you ask Jake about the throw?" I asked.

"No," Jessica replied with a guarded shrug. "He stayed in his room for most of the night. I hardly saw him."

"You mean, he didn't have a big fight with you at nine o'clock over whether you were going to watch your favorite show, *Nature's Parade* or his favorite show, *The Usual Suspects?*"

Jessica looked startled. "How did you know those were our favorite shows?"

"You'd be amazed at what I know about you and Jake."

The other kids started to come in. I looked in Mr. Dirksen's desk and found his attendance book. After I took attendance, the kids listened to announcements over the PA, and I looked through

40

Mr. Dirksen's schedule. He had to teach a sixth-grade gifted and talented science class next period, then he had study hall, then he was supposed to teach my class.

The bell rang and the eighth-graders got up to leave. Jessica picked up her book bag and started out of the room.

"Uh, Jessica, could you wait for a moment?" I said.

"I'll be late for gym," she said.

"Don't worry. I'll give you a pass." I waited until the other kids left the room. "So, I guess Jake had to do the dinner dishes last night."

Jessica made a face. "How'd you know that?"

"Well, it was your turn, but he bet you yesterday you couldn't throw a football as far as you did. You made him look like a jerk in front of his friends as usual, but that's nothing new."

Jessica stared at me. "How do you know all this stuff, Mr. Dirksen?"

"You mean, how do I know about the love letters from that dweeb, Danny, you met at camp last year? The ones that are stashed in the third drawer of your dresser behind your sweaters? Or that you've got forty-two dollars and twenty-seven cents stuffed in the toe of your left soccer shoe in your closet? Or how about the half-finished, giant-size bag of M&M's behind the row of paperbacks on your bookshelf?"

41

Jessica's jaw dropped and her eyes went wide. "Ohmygod!" she gasped, staring at me like I was an alien or something.

"Listen," I said. "I don't want you to be late for gym. But tonight, why don't you ask Jake what you did to him the time he put the dead frog in your sneaker. Or maybe you could remind him of the time you and your friend Sophie glued his baseball mitt closed. See if he remembers how he got revenge for *that* move."

Jessica just stared at me with wide, frightened eyes. "There's no way you could know about that stuff, Mr. Dirksen," she said, backing slowly out of the room.

"Talk to Jake tonight," I said. "Then let's talk tomorrow."

The first sixth-grade science class I taught were the gifted and talented brains, so I just told them to read as far as they could in their science text books. Those kids were so dumb they actually did it.

Study hall was a snap, too. Everyone just sat around and read or did homework. I was starting to think that being a teacher wasn't so tough after all.

Finally, it was time for my class. Jake, I mean, Mr. Dirksen came in wearing my gray dress-up slacks and an ugly blue and brown check shirt my

Aunt Elma had given me for my birthday. I'd never even taken it out of the box. He'd greased my hair down and parted it on the wrong side. It really hurt to see me looking like such a dork.

"Jake, will you come up here, please," I said.

Jake, I mean, Mr. Dirksen walked up to the front of the room while the other kids were still settling into their seats.

"When are you going to tell my parents the truth?" I whispered.

He just shrugged. "Maybe never."

"You can't do that," I hissed. "It's not fair."

"Why not?" he said in a low voice. "It's fun being a kid again. Besides, there's nothing you can do about it."

Boy, he made me mad. "Well, as long as you're going to be me, would you mind not wearing clothes like that? You're making me look like an idiot!"

Jake, I mean, Mr. Dirksen looked down at my clothes and frowned. "They were in your closet."

"Yeah, but it's stuff my mother and aunt bought me," I said. "Not stuff I'd ever wear."

"Well, everything else in your closet was jeans and sweat shirts," he said.

"Because that's what *normal* kids wear," I said.

Jake, I mean, Mr. Dirksen and I stared at each other for a moment.

"I assume you stayed in my house last night,"

he said in a low voice. "Did you remember to turn off the lights and lock the door before you came to school this morning?"

"Maybe," I whispered. "But if you come to school dressed like that tomorrow, I'm definitely leaving everything on."

By now most of the class had taken their seats.

"You better have the class read a chapter in their science texts," Mr. Dirksen whispered. "I don't want them to fall any further behind than they already are."

"Don't tell me what to do," I said irritably. "You're just a kid."

"Do you want to get your fellow students into trouble?" Mr. Dirksen asked.

"Go back to your seat," I said.

He went back to his seat and I stood up before the class. Almost immediately, Amanda Gluck started to cough.

"Amanda," I said. "You may go out and get a drink of water."

Amanda pushed her glasses back up on her nose and looked surprised. "Are you sure, Mr. Dirksen?"

"Yes." I looked at the rest of the class. "Does anyone have to use the bathroom?"

Three hands went up.

"Go right ahead," I said.

Amanda and the others left the room. I turned

back to the class. "Class, today we're going to learn how to make a bomb."

The kids all looked at each other in disbelief. A hand shot up. It belonged to Jake, er, I mean, Mr. Dirksen. "Uh, excuse me, Mr. Dirksen. But don't you think that might be dangerous?"

"Jake," I said. "Please go to the blackboard and write, *I will not ask stupid questions* one hundred times."

"But, Mr. Dirksen," he gasped.

"You'd better hurry or you'll have to write it two hundred times."

Jake got up and slammed his chair under his desk angrily. Then he went up to the blackboard and started to write.

"All right, class," I said. "Does anyone know the chemical formula for gunpowder?"

A boy named Howie Jamison raised his hand. "Potassium nitrate, powdered charcoal, and sulfur."

The chemicals were locked in the glass cabinets that lined the wall. I took Mr. Dirksen's keys out of my pocket and opened them. Inside, we found everything we needed.

What a blast! By the end of the class, kids were making fire crackers, Roman candles, and sparklers. Almost everyone went out for water or to the bathroom at least once, and a couple of kids didn't even bother to come back. I was in the middle of going through Mr. Dirksen's desk when Andy and Josh came up.

"Uh, excuse us, Mr. Dirksen," Andy said.

"Yes?"

"We were wondering if we could make a really big bomb," Josh said. "Like maybe the size of a football, or something."

"Why?" I asked.

"Well, we thought we could bury it in the ground and see how big a hole we could blow up," Andy said.

"I think that shows exceptional thinking for a couple of retards like yourselves," I said. "Unfortunately, your project would use up all the remaining chemicals, and I need them so that the other sixth-grade classes can make bombs as well."

Josh and Andy looked disappointed. They went back to their desks and built a medium-size bomb. I was having so much fun that I was sorry when the bell rang. Mr. Dirksen was still writing *I will not ask stupid questions* on the blackboard.

"I hope you're proud of yourself," he sputtered after everyone had left.

"If you don't like it, give me my body back," I said.

Mr. Dirksen thought for a moment, then shook his head.

My good mood quickly vanished. "You can't stay me forever. I mean, it's totally unfair."

"Maybe I don't care what you think," Mr. Dirksen said.

"Oh, yeah?" I said. "Then you better plan on writing on the blackboard every time you walk in here. And I'll probably fail you, too."

"Big deal." Mr. Dirksen shrugged and walked out of the classroom. I couldn't believe how much he reminded me of me.

Bomb-making ruled for the rest of the day. Anyone who wanted to get a drink of water, or use the bathroom, or just didn't feel like being in class was excused. It was kind of fun, until the end of the day when I realized I had no place to go except Mr. Dirksen's house. That was a bummer.

I dismissed my last class and sat at Mr. Dirksen's desk, wondering what to do. The room was a mess. Open jars of chemicals and half-finished bombs lay all over the place. Someone knocked on the door.

"Who is it?" I asked.

Jessica pushed open the door and stuck her head in. "Can I come in?"

"It's a free country," I said.

Jessica walked slowly toward me, staring like she didn't know what to expect.

"I talked to Jake," she said.

"And?"

"He looked like Jake, but he doesn't act like

Jake. He didn't even know the nickname we used to call Grandma before she died."

"Gaba gaba," I said.

Jessica just stared at me. "I don't believe this."

"You're not the only one."

Jessica shook her head. "It's not possible."

"When Dad clips his toenails, he always leaves the shavings on his night table and Mom always yells at him about it," I said. "When you were ten you rode your bike into the sliding glass door next to the kitchen and had to get fourteen stitches. Last year at Christmas, Aunt Elma sent you a Barbie doll and you said she was senile. You were the flower girl at Cousin Judy's wedding when you were seven. I was five and they made me the ring bearer, except I thought I was the ring bear, like this furry animal with rings. Want me to keep going?"

The color drained out of Jessica's face. "How did it happen?"

I explained about Mr. Dirksen's experiment and the thunderstorm again.

"But it's impossible," she said.

"That's what I thought."

My sister took a deep breath. "Okay," she said. "Here's the clincher. When I was eight and Jake was six, something happened that involved our neighbor Mr. Rooney's bedroom window and a baseball. Jake and I swore we'd keep it a secret forever. What was it?"

"It's a trick question," I said. "We didn't have a neighbor named Rooney when you were eight. The Lusks lived on one side of us and the Grodnicks lived on the other side. The Grodnicks didn't move out until you were ten. That's when the Rooneys moved in. And anyway, it was the Lusks' window I broke with the baseball."

Jessica's skin turned paler. "Jake?" she whispered.

"You got him," I answered with a nod. "Jake Sherman in a dork's body."

"What are you going to do?" Jessica asked.

Before I could answer, the door opened again. Principal Blanco came in, looking stern. "Phil," he said. "I'd like to have a word with you."

8

Jessica and I stared at each other nervously.

"Oh, sorry," Principal Blanco said. "I wasn't interrupting anything, was I?"

"Uh . . ." I wasn't sure how to answer.

"No, no, of course not," Jessica said quickly. "Mr. Dirksen and I were just talking about a homework assignment. I'll wait outside until you're done."

She hurried toward the door and pulled it closed behind her, leaving me alone with Principal Blanco. Principal Blanco crossed his arms and looked sternly at me. He was a short, pudgy man with curly black hair and deep wrinkles in his forehead.

"Phil," he said, "how long have we known each other?"

"Uh . . ."

"A long time," Principal Blanco said with a nod. "Nearly twelve years. You came in as a science teacher. Do you remember what I started as?"

"Uh . . ."

"A phys ed teacher, that's right," Blanco nodded again. "I worked hard, Phil. All the way up to principal. And do you know why they made me principal?"

"Uh, because everyone was afraid of you?" I guessed.

Principal Blanco smiled. "That's funny, Phil. In all these years I never knew you had a sense of humor. No, the reason they made me principal was because I followed the rules. I did what was expected of me, and I didn't let anyone get out of line. Now, do you know why I'm standing here right now?"

"I let too many kids go to the bathroom at the same time?"

Blanco smiled and shook his head. "Still with the jokes. The reason I'm here is because there's a rumor going around that you were teaching bomb-making in your class today."

Principal Blanco paused and looked around the room at all the half-finished bombs and open jars of chemicals. "Looks like the kids have been pretty busy today. What was the project?"

"Bombs," I said.

Principal Blanco grinned. "You've turned into a regular comedian. But seriously, Phil, you're one teacher I've always respected. I like your no-

nonsense attitude. I admit some parents have complained about your policy of not allowing kids to use the bathroom or get a drink of water. Other parents say you give too much homework. But I've always said, let the man do his job the best way he sees fit. And if that means the kids have to hold it in until after class is over, so be it."

I nodded.

"I just wanted to make sure we were still on the same wavelength," Principal Blanco said.

I nodded again.

"Good." Principal Blanco headed for the door. "Now tomorrow, let's get back on track."

Principal Blanco went out and Jessica came back in.

"What was that all about?" she asked.

"I'm not sure," I said. "I think it was about making bombs in class today. But it might have been about not letting kids go to the bathroom."

Jessica scowled. "You made bombs in class today?"

"Sure. Why not?"

"Do you want to get fired?" my sister asked.

"Uh, I don't know," I said. "Do I?"

"Of course not! If Mr. Dirksen gets fired he might have to move away," Jessica said. "Then you'll never get your body back."

I hadn't thought of that.

"Look, let's get out of here," Jessica said. "We have to figure out what to do."

*   *   *

A few minutes later, out on the sidewalk, Jessica made a left as if she were heading home.

"Where are you going?" I asked.

"Home," Jessica said. "Oh, right. We can't go there. Mom and Dad would freak. Where are you going?"

"Home. I mean, Mr. Dirksen's home."

"Okay," Jessica said. "I'll go with you. I really want to see this experiment anyway."

We started down the sidewalk.

"Look," Jessica said. "We have to figure out a way to get you and Mr. Dirksen to switch bodies again."

"Are you sure?" I asked. "Maybe Mr. Dirksen would make a better Jake than me. I mean, you're always telling me what a pain I am."

"You may be a pain, but Mr. Dirksen is turning Jake into a nerd," my sister said. "Not only did he do the dishes last night, but he swept the kitchen floor and took out the garbage. He even straightened the dishes in the kitchen cabinets."

"So what's so bad about that?"

"Simple," Jessica said. "You know how Mom and Dad are always saying they wish you were more like me? Well, last night, for the first time ever, Mom said she wished I could be more like you."

"It's that bad, huh?"

Jessica nodded. "Frankly, given the choice between having a pain or a nerd for a brother, I'll go with the pain."

"I consider that a true vote of support," I said.

"Don't," Jessica said. "Believe me, if I figure out a way to get you guys switched back, you're gonna owe me big time."

"I promise I'll wash the dishes forever."

"Don't do me any favors," Jessica muttered. "Now the first thing we have to do is get Mr. Dirksen to agree to switch back."

"Forget it," I said.

"Why?"

"Because he *likes* being me. He thinks it's better than being him. And frankly, he's right. I mean, how would you like to have this body?"

Jessica gave me a look from head to toe. "You're right. I'd hate it."

"It's hopeless," I said sadly. "I'm gonna spend the rest of my life trapped in my teacher's body. Do you realize how unfair this is? I'm not ever going to get to be a *teenager*!"

"You better get hold of yourself," Jessica warned.

I tried, but suddenly the future looked really bleak.

"That's easy for you to say!" I cried. "You still have a chance to ditch school and lie to Mom and Dad about where you've been all day. You'll get to go to sleepaway camp and sit in the back of the bus on field trips and make faces at the other

54

drivers. You'll experience the joy of getting your driver's license and being able to bomb around town with the radio turned up as high as you like. . . . What do I have to look forward to?"

Jessica thought for a moment. "You can vote."

I glared at her in disbelief. "Drop dead, Jessica."

We got to Mr. Dirksen's house. I opened the garage door and showed Jessica the experiment.

"Incredible," she whispered, walking around it. "He actually figured out a way to switch bodies."

"He was only trying to transfer intelligence from smart animals to dumb animals," I explained. "But then lightning struck and all the extra electricity made us switch bodies."

"Does that mean you'll need lightning to change you back?" Jessica asked.

"I don't know," I said. "But that's not the problem right now. The problem is I can't get Mr. Dirksen to *agree* to switch."

"Hmmmm." Jessica put a thick strand of hair in her mouth and chewed on it, which was what she did when she was thinking. "We know that Mr. Dirksen actually likes being you. I can probably do something about that. But in the meantime we're also going to have to try to make Mr. Dirksen want to be himself again."

"Why would he want to do that?" I asked. "He knows he's a totally boring teacher and everyone hates him. He has a bad back and is nearly blind as a bat. Not only that, even in jeans he still looks like a total basket case."

Jessica stared at me and her eyes went wide. "That's it! Maybe we can do something about that, too."

9

The next morning I was pulling on Mr. Dirk-sen's jeans when the doorbell rang. It was probably Jessica, hurrying over before school to make some last minute changes in her plan to help me get my body back. I tucked in the heavy denim shirt we'd bought at the mall the night before. Jessica had picked it out because she said it made Mr. Dirksen's shoulders look wider.

Briinnggg! The doorbell rang again.

"Coming!" As I walked to the door, I pulled on the white baseball cap we'd bought to cover Mr. Dirksen's bald head.

I pulled the door open, but Jessica wasn't outside. Ms. Rogers was. She was holding a brown paper grocery bag.

"Phil!" she gasped. Once again her big blue eyes went wide as she stared at me. "You shaved off your beard!"

I nodded and ran my hand along my smooth jaw. Jessica had helped me shave the night before.

"And how can you see without your glasses?" Ms. Rogers asked.

"Contacts," I said. We'd gotten a set of disposable ones from the optometrist in the mall. It turned out there were a *few* advantages to being thirty-five and owning a credit card.

Ms. Rogers just stood there and stared. "I can't believe it's really you."

"It's the *new* me," I said, puffing out Mr. Dirksen's chest. "The me every thirty-five-year-old science teacher wishes he could be. So what do you think?"

"I, I think you look very handsome!" Ms. Rogers blurted.

"Well, thanks, Ms. Rogers, er . . . I mean, Kim. You look pretty terrific yourself."

Ms. Rogers blushed, and then stared up at me. "How did you get so tan?"

"I went for a long jog yesterday after work," I said. "I guess the sun was out." The truth was, Jessica had also taken me to a tanning salon the night before. Then she smeared some stuff on my skin that made me look even tanner.

"You went jogging?" Ms. Rogers gave me an amazed look.

"Absolutely," I said. "It's part of my new fitness regimen."

Ms. Rogers seemed to be at a loss for words.

"So what's in the bag?" I asked.

"Oh, I stopped at the store and got you some

things. I knew you wouldn't be able to shop without a car."

"Why, that's so nice of you, Kim," I said. "Why don't you come in?"

Ms. Rogers stepped into the house. She stared into the living room at the wrinkled blanket and sheets on the couch and the empty Domino's box and soda bottles.

"Something wrong?" I asked.

"Uh, no, nothing." Ms. Rogers quickly shook her head. "Have you had breakfast yet?"

"Actually, I was just thinking about fixing myself something," I said, walking toward the kitchen.

"Well, if you haven't started yet, I'd be glad to make something for you," Ms. Rogers said as she followed.

"I'd love that," I said. "You know, the breakfast you made yesterday was one of the best I've ever eaten."

Ms. Rogers turned to me. Her lower lip quivered slightly. "Do you really mean that, Phil?"

"With all my heart," I said.

Ms. Rogers practically danced into the kitchen. *If only Josh and Andy could see this*, I thought with a grin.

Ms. Rogers made me breakfast, then sat down across from me while I ate.

"You've really changed, Phil," she said. "You're

so much more, uh, lively than the way you used to be. And you're dressing differently and acting differently. You're just, uh, so much more *youthful*. Has something happened that you haven't told me about?"

"Not really," I said.

Ms. Rogers leaned across the table toward me. "Come on, Phil, you can tell me."

"Well," I said. "It's just that it's not something I talk a lot about, you know? I mean, especially with people I haven't known that long."

"I don't understand," Ms. Rogers said with a frown.

"Well, you and I," I tried to explain.

"Phil, I've known you since I was seven years old," Ms. Rogers said. "You used to date my big sister, Ellen."

"I did?" I asked. "I mean, yes, Ellen. . . . We used to date, sure."

"Don't tell me you've forgotten," Ms. Rogers said.

"Oh, no, of course not. How is Ellen, anyway? I never see her around anymore."

Again, Ms. Rogers frowned. "Don't you remember? She entered the convent. She's a nun."

"A nun," I repeated. "A nun! Oh, right. Sure. I knew that."

Ms. Rogers gave me a funny look. "Are you sure you're feeling all right, Phil?"

"Well, uh, I'm always a little lightheaded until I've had breakfast," I said.

"I'm starting to see that," Ms. Rogers said. "Anyway, how's your experiment coming along?"

"My experiment?" I repeated nervously.

"Don't tell me you've forgotten about that, too," Ms. Rogers said with a laugh.

"Oh, no, no, of course not. It's coming along very nicely."

"Did you get the thing you were waiting for?" she asked. "They were going to ship it to you. What did you call it?"

"Uh . . ." I'd forgotten now what Mr. Dirksen had called it. A *something*scope. *Tele*scope? No. *Micro*scope? Of course not. A *stethoscope?* Maybe.

"Do you mean the stethoscope?"

"Stethoscope?" Ms. Rogers frowned. "I thought that was something a doctor used to listen to hearts."

"Oh, right," I said quickly. "Turned out I needed one of those, too."

Ms. Rogers was giving me funny looks again. I knew I had to change the subject fast.

"You know what I've been meaning to ask you, uh, Kim?" I said. "There's a young man in one of my classes. His name is Jake Sherman. Do you know him?"

Ms. Rogers smiled and nodded. "I call him my favorite troublemaker."

"Well, I'm a little bit worried about him," I said.

"Why? Is something wrong?" Ms. Rogers suddenly looked concerned.

"Apparently there's been a case of bubonic plague in his family."

"Bubonic plague!" Ms. Rogers gasped.

I nodded seriously. "No one's supposed to know about it. The doctors are *pretty* sure it hasn't spread to any of the other family members, but it's such a terribly contagious disease that I just felt it best to warn you not to get too close. There's no cure, you know."

Ms. Rogers stared at me with a shocked expression on her face. "Well, thank you for telling me, Phil. I'll make sure I don't get too close to him."

I finished breakfast, and Ms. Rogers gave me a ride to school. I just hoped Jessica's plan would work.

According to my sister's plan, I had to change things when my class showed up that day. Of course, Jake, I mean, Mr. Dirksen was the first person to walk into the room after the bell rang. This time he stopped in the doorway and stared at me.

"What have you done to me?" he gasped.

"You like it?"

"You shaved off my beard! And where are my glasses?"

"Didn't feel like wearing them today."

"How can you see anything?"

"Contacts."

"You got me contacts?" Jake, I mean, Mr. Dirksen asked, amazed.

"With *your* credit card," I said.

"That's fraud!" he gasped.

"Prove it."

Mr. Dirksen gritted my teeth and crossed the room to sit down at my desk. He was wearing my dress slacks again. Today he'd added a blue long-sleeved polo shirt buttoned up to the neck. I never knew I could look like such a nerd.

Now Andy and Josh came in.

"Yo, Mr. Dirksen, lookin' good!" Andy shouted, pumping his fist.

"Way to go, dude!" Josh agreed. "I like the hat."

"Please be seated, boys," I said.

The rest of the class came in and took their seats.

"So what are we gonna do today?" Andy asked. "Make more bombs?"

"I say we make a rocket today," Josh said. "Like a really big one. And we take a mouse or something and put it inside."

"Yeah, the first mousetronaut!" Andy shouted.

"Please calm down," I said. "I have an announcement to make."

Amanda Gluck raised her hand. "Mr. Dirksen, can I get a drink?"

"In just a moment, Amanda," I said.

"But I'm really thirsty," she said.

"Please wait until I make my announcement," I said.

"Booo!" Josh shouted.

"Hisss!" Andy joined in.

"It's the old Mr. Dirksen again!" Josh yelled.

"Would you please be quiet!" I said, getting annoyed.

I happened to glance at Mr. Dirksen. He gave me a smug smile as if to say, *See?*

"We want the new Mr. Dirksen!" Andy yelled.

The next thing I knew, the whole class was chanting, *"We want the new Mr. Dirksen! We want the new Mr. Dirksen!"*

"Listen," I said, raising my voice. "I just want to make an announcement."

"We want the new Mr. Dirksen! We want the new Mr. Dirksen!" the class kept shouting.

"Will you phlegmwads shut up!" I shouted.

The whole class stared at me in stunned silence. Finally Josh raised his hand. "Excuse me, sir, but did you just call us phlegmwads?"

"That is indeed what I called you," I replied.

"Well, sir, I don't recall you ever using that kind of language before," Josh said. The rest of the class began to grin.

"That's true, Josh," I replied. "But it seemed necessary in order to get you pea-brained dirt bags settled down long enough to listen to my announcement."

Now Andy's hand went up. "But sir, does this mean you're still the new Mr. Dirksen?"

"That it does," I said with a nod. The class began to clap, but I waved my arm. "Now I would like to get on with my announcement so that Amanda can get her water. Today we will not be making bombs. We will return to the chapters I last assigned you."

"Aw, boo." The class looked unhappy.

Julia Saks raised her hand. "But you said you're not the old Mr. Dirksen anymore. You're not going to start giving us boring lectures again like you used to, are you?"

"No," I said. "First we are going to review what you've read and then we are going to do an experiment."

Now a new hand shot up. It belonged to me.

"Yes, Mr. Dirk — er, I mean, Jake?"

"Do you really think it's wise to do another experiment after the mess we made yesterday?" he asked.

"Please go to the blackboard, Jake," I said, holding out a new piece of chalk, "and write *I will not ask stupid questions* one hundred times."

While Jake wrote on the blackboard, the class and I reviewed the various human organs involved in eating and drinking.

"And what is the tube called that takes the food from the mouth to the stomach?" I asked, reading from Mr. Dirksen's class notes.

"The esophagus," someone said.

"And what makes the food go down?" I asked.

"Gravity?" someone asked.

"No," I said. "Gravity has nothing to do with it. There is a series of muscular contractions that force food down the esophagus. Does anyone know what they're called?"

Another hand went up. "Peristaltic waves?"

"That's correct," I said. "And that is why astronauts in space can eat."

Josh raised his hand. "Well, if you're in space and you eat something, maybe the peristaltic waves get it down there, but what keeps it down there?"

"Yeah," said Andy. "Why doesn't all that chewed up, half-digested space food just come bubbling back up into your mouth?"

"Uh . . ." I read quickly through Mr. Dirksen's notes, looking for an answer, but I couldn't find one.

"Uh, Mr. Dirksen?"

I turned and found that Jake, I mean, Mr. Dirksen had turned from the blackboard.

"Yes, Jake?" I said.

"I think the answer is that when the esophagus is not in use, it collapses like a flattened straw and doesn't allow the food to come back up."

"Uh, good answer, Jake," I said. "Now keep writing."

Jake, I mean, Mr. Dirksen turned back to the

blackboard and I turned back to the class. "Did everybody hear that?"

The students nodded.

Now Josh's hand went up again. "I thought you said we were gonna do an experiment."

"Uh, we are," I said. The problem was, I didn't know what the experiment would be. Then I had an idea. "Let's try to prove that peristaltic waves exist and that getting food or liquids to the stomach has nothing to do with gravity."

"You mean, go into space and eat some food?" Andy asked.

"I don't think so," I said. "Does anyone have any ideas on how we can prove peristaltic waves exist?"

Barry Dunn raised his hand. Barry had shaved his head almost completely bald, except for one long blond lock that grew from the back of his head down between his shoulders. He always wore black T-shirts, black jeans, and black lace-up boots. This was the first time I had ever seen him raise his hand.

"Yes, Barry?" I said.

"We could give somebody something to eat," he said. "Then we could cut them open and actually watch the peristaltic waves do their thing."

"Excellent idea," I said. "Does anyone want to volunteer to be cut open?"

No hands went up. Barry looked very disappointed.

"Sorry, Barry," I said. "Looks like we'll have to ask for other suggestions."

Amanda Gluck raised her hand. "Maybe we could get someone to stand on his head and drink a glass of water. If peristaltic waves exist, then the water should still go to that person's stomach even though they're upside down."

"Great idea!" I said. "Now who would like to be the volunteer?"

Once again, not a single hand went up. The kids in the class glanced at each other nervously.

"Doesn't anyone want to be the guinea pig?" I asked.

Everyone shook their heads. Just then there was a loud, awful *screech!* as Mr. Dirksen broke a piece of chalk while writing. Everyone covered their ears with their hands.

"Sorry," Mr. Dirksen said sheepishly.

Suddenly I got the most excellent idea. "Jake, you just volunteered."

10

Jake, I mean, Mr. Dirksen turned pale. "Stand on my head and drink water?"

"Through a straw," I said, turning back to the class. "Andy, go out and get a cup of water. Josh, go find a straw."

Josh and Andy left the room. Now another kid raised his hand. "This is dumb, Mr. Dirksen. No one can drink water while standing on his head."

"Does everyone feel that way?" I asked.

About half the hands in the room went up.

"So half of you think it's impossible," I said. "And the other half thinks it's possible. Tell you what. Let's have a bet. Everyone put up a quarter."

Just then, Andy and Josh came back into the room with a cup of water and a straw.

"Hey, what's going on?" Josh asked.

"Mr. Dirksen said we could bet a quarter on whether Jake can drink upside down or not," Barry Dunn said.

"Cool," Josh quickly reached into his pocket. "How about fifty cents? Will anyone go up to a dollar?"

The next thing I knew, I had a regular casino going. Josh was even making side bets. "I'll lay six to one odds Jake barfs. Who wants to take the barf bet?"

Finally we were ready. All except for Jake, I mean, Mr. Dirksen.

"I don't think I can do this," he whimpered.

"Listen, barf breath, I got a lot of money riding on this," Josh threatened. "You're going to do it."

"But I can't stand on my head," he said.

Josh and Andy glanced at each other and nodded.

"We'll help you," Andy said.

They both grabbed one of Jake's legs. Barry Dunn and another guy grabbed the other leg. They held him upside down with his head about two inches above the floor.

"Someone slide the cup and straw to his mouth," I said.

Julia held the cup steady while Amanda positioned the straw in Jake's mouth. The rest of the class crowded around and watched eagerly.

"Okay, Jake," I shouted. "Drink!"

He took a tentative sip.

"*Blech!*" He shook his head and grabbed his nose. A little water ran out of it.

"What happened?" Josh asked.

"The water came out his nose," I said. "Does anyone know how the water got from his mouth to his nose?"

"Through his nasal passage," someone said.

Still hanging upside down, Jake kept snorting.

"And what's the flap of skin called that's supposed to stop food from going up into the nasal passage?" I asked.

"The uvula," someone said.

"Right," I said.

"So how come the water went into Jake's nose?" Andy asked.

"Obviously Jake has a malfunctioning uvula," I said.

"Could you please let me go?" Jake groaned, upside down.

"No way," Josh said. "I got a lot of money riding on this. Try again."

"But it just runs out my nose," Jake complained.

"Julia," I said. "Hold Jake's nose."

With Julia holding Jake's, I mean, Mr. Dirksen's nose, he took another sip.

And then another.

And another!

Soon the whole cup was empty!

"He did it!" Josh shouted, letting go of Jake's leg. Jake landed in a heap on the floor while Andy and Josh went around the room collecting their winnings. Meanwhile, I went up to the front of the room to sum up what we'd learned that day.

"So what is the tube that takes food from the mouth to the stomach?" I asked.

"The esophagus," someone said.

"And what are the muscle contractions that move the food down to the stomach called?"

"Peristaltic waves," someone answered.

"And why doesn't the food come back up once it's in the stomach?"

"Because the esophagus collapses like a flattened straw and won't let it," someone said.

The bell rang. "Class dismissed," I said.

The class filed out. When everyone had gone, Jake, I mean, Mr. Dirksen stopped at my desk. His hair was a mess, and the front of his shirt was all wet.

"Very funny," he muttered.

"Hey, at least we learned something today," I said.

Jake, I mean, Mr. Dirksen just glared at me for a moment.

"Listen," I said. "Any time you want to switch back, just say the word."

Mr. Dirksen shook his head and started to walk out.

"Hey, wait a minute," I said. "Remember before when they asked me that question about why food didn't come back up in space? How come you answered?"

Jake, I mean, Mr. Dirksen stopped in the doorway. "Because I didn't want them to think that you, I mean, that *I* didn't know the answer."

The rest of the day went pretty well. We did all kinds of demonstrations and experiments in my classes, and I felt pretty good until I remembered that I was supposed to be a student, not the teacher.

Finally the last bell of the day rang. I sat at Mr. Dirksen's desk and stared at the empty classroom. The last thing in the world I wanted to do was go back to Mr. Dirksen's dismal house.

There was a knock on the door, and Jessica came in.

"How'd it go?" she asked, sitting on the edge of Mr. Dirksen's desk.

"Great . . . er, I mean, terrible," I said. "I had Jake hang upside down and drink water until it ran out of his nose and he *still* doesn't want to be Mr. Dirksen again."

"Wow, he must've really hated being himself," Jessica said.

"I can see why. How are things going at home?"

"Mom and Dad keep going around saying Jake's not acting like himself," Jessica said. "I'm doing everything I can to drive him crazy, but it's like he knows what I'm up to and he won't let it bother him."

I shook my head sadly. "This is bad, Jessica.

It's really starting to look like I'm going to spend the rest of my life being a nerdy middle school science teacher with a bad back."

Jessica patted me on the shoulder. "Well, look at it this way. At least you won't have me bothering you."

11

The next day was the same. Ms. Rogers stopped by to make me breakfast and drive me to school. She was really sweet and nice, and we laughed a lot. Seeing her in the morning was the high point of my day. In class we did more experiments and demonstrations. The kids learned a lot, but they had a lot of fun, too. I knew it was bugging Jake, I mean, Mr. Dirksen that I could be a better teacher than he was. But he still didn't say anything about switching back.

On Wednesday morning, while driving me to school, Ms. Rogers asked me if I could do lunch duty for her that day.

"I hate to impose, Phil," she said, "but I have to meet with a parent today. She works in town, and sixth-grade lunch is the only time we're both free."

"Sure, I'd be glad to help out," I said.

Ms. Rogers drove into the parking lot and parked her car. Then she turned and smiled at me. "You're such a sweet man, Phil." The next thing I knew, she leaned over and kissed me on the cheek.

At sixth-grade lunch I stood in the cafeteria and watched the kids come out of the lunch line. Josh and Andy came out and went over to our regular table. Where was Jake, I mean, Mr. Dirksen? I looked around and spotted him sitting by himself at a table in the corner.

I went over to Josh and Andy. "Hey, guys."

"Hey, Mr. Dirksen," they both said with their mouths half-filled with food.

"So how're you guys doing?" I asked.

"Okay." Josh nodded. "You gonna give us a quiz on Friday?"

That's right! I'd forgotten that Mr. Dirksen gave the class a quiz every Friday.

"I think we'll skip it this week."

"All right!" Josh and Andy gave each other high-fives.

Then Andy looked up at me wondrously. "I hope you don't mind me saying this, Mr. Dirksen, but I don't get it. You used to be such a bogus dude. Now you're one of the coolest teachers in the school. What happened?"

"I guess I just changed," I said.

"Just like that, huh?" Andy said.

I nodded and glanced back at Jake sitting by himself. "Let me ask you a question. You two and Jake Sherman used to be like the Three Muske-

76

teers. You were always together. How come Jake's sitting over there by himself?"

Josh and Andy glanced at each other.

"Did something happen?" I asked.

"He's just no fun anymore," Andy said. "Like we want to fool around, and all he wants to do is read and stuff. I mean, look at him."

We all looked over at Jake. He was still sitting by himself, but now he'd opened a book.

"It's like all of a sudden he changed into this totally boring dweeb," Josh said. "I don't know what happened. He's just boring."

Josh's words sent a pang deep through me. These were my best friends, and they didn't like me anymore! Josh and Andy finished their lunches.

"Come on," Andy said, picking up his football. "Let's go outside and have a catch."

"Maybe you could ask Jake to join you," I said.

Josh shook his head. "You know how many times I've asked him to have a catch in the last few days? He's hopeless."

Josh and Andy went out to the playground. I walked over to the table where Jake was reading and pulled up a chair.

"Uh, excuse me," I said.

Jake looked up from his book. When he saw me, he frowned. "What do you want?"

"I want to know why you've stopped hanging around with my best friends," I said.

"Because they're infantile troublemakers," Jake answered with a shrug.

"Well, maybe that's true," I said, "but they're still my friends. And you're not gonna blow that for me."

"Don't tell me what to do," Jake snapped and looked back into his book. That really made me mad. I reached over and tipped the book down until our eyes met again.

"Listen," I said. "You better stay friendly with my friends or I'm gonna go to the mall tonight and charge about ten thousand dollars worth of junk on your credit card. And then I'll have a huge party at your house and invite all the kids in the neighborhood."

"You wouldn't dare," gasped Jake, I mean, Mr. Dirksen.

"Try me."

Jake, I mean, Mr. Dirksen sighed and closed his book. "If you want me to have friends, you might stop spreading stupid rumors about me. The nurse stopped me in the hall today. Couldn't you come up with something better than bubonic plague?"

I grinned sheepishly. I'd forgotten about that. "Okay, no more rumors."

Jake nodded wearily. "So, where are your friends?"

"Outside, throwing a football around."

"Wonderful," Jake muttered. But he got up and went outside. Through the window I watched him join Josh and Andy and go out for a pass. He dropped it, but at least he was playing.

On Thursday we did another experiment. Just before the end of class, Principal Blanco came in. "Phil, can I speak to you out in the hall for a minute?"

I felt the blood drain out of my, I mean, Mr. Dirksen's face. What had I done? I glanced at Jake, sitting at my desk. He just shrugged like he had no idea what Principal Blanco could want.

"Uh, class," I said, "the period's almost over. Please finish up your experiments."

Then I went out in the hall. Principal Blanco crossed his thick arms. "I've noticed that you've been coming to school dressed very casually, Phil."

I looked down at my jeans and denim shirt and swallowed. "That's true, sir."

"I've also heard that you're creating quite a commotion in your classes," he said. "Sometimes I can hear the noise clear down at the end of the hall."

"Uh, yes, that's probably true," I said. Jessica's words came back to haunt me. *If Mr. Dirksen gets fired he might have to move away. Then you'll never get your body back.*

"It's a rather dramatic change from the way you used to conduct your classes, wouldn't you say?" Principal Blanco asked.

"Uh, yes."

Principal Blanco stared straight at me. I wondered if I should get down on my knees and beg him for another chance.

"I've decided to use you to set an example," Principal Blanco said.

I bit Mr. Dirksen's lip and felt his stomach tighten.

Ohmygod! I thought. *I've blown it. He's gonna fire me!*

"Tomorrow I'm bringing a group of visiting teachers in to observe your class," he said.

I could just see them all standing at the back of the classroom, trying to decide if they wanted to take my job or not.

"Mr. Blanco, please don't," I begged. "I know things have been pretty weird in my class, but there's a reason for it. It's just that if I tried to explain, you'd never believe me."

"Wouldn't believe what?" Principal Blanco asked.

"Well, just what's happened," I said. "You see, Mr. Dirksen had this experiment . . . er, I mean, *I* had this experiment. And it just changed everything."

"I know you've been doing a lot of experiments," Principal Blanco said.

"I'll stop if you want," I said. "I mean, I can

always go back to those boring lectures Mr. Dirksen, I mean, I used to give."

Principal Blanco frowned. "But you don't want to do that."

"I don't?"

"Of course not," the principal said. "Why do you think I'm having teachers observe your class? I want them to learn from you, Phil. You're doing a wonderful job."

Suddenly I was confused. "I am?"

"Absolutely. The kids are learning. They're excited. They're making noise. Other teachers keep stopping me in the hall and asking me what you've done."

"They do?" I was stunned.

"Now you just keep doing exactly what you've been doing, Phil," Principal Blanco said and slapped me on the shoulder. "Keep up the good work."

Just then the bell rang and my students came out of the class.

"Have a good day, Mr. Dirksen!"

"See you tomorrow, Mr. Dirksen!"

Josh and Andy came out. "So what kind of experiment are we gonna do tomorrow?" Andy asked.

"Well, I haven't decided yet," I said. "We're studying the solutions produced by the glands in the stomach, so maybe we'll dissolve some stuff in acid."

"Way cool!" Andy gasped.

"Man, I never thought science could be so much fun!" Josh said. "See you tomorrow, Mr. Dirksen."

I watched my two friends disappear into the crowds of students moving down the hall to their next class. *Wow*, I thought. *This can't be happening!*

"Uh, Mr. Dirksen?"

I turned around. Jake, I mean, Mr. Dirksen was standing behind me. "Yeah?"

"What did Alan want?"

"Who?"

"Alan Blanco, the principal of this school."

"He wanted to commend me on how much my teaching had improved," I said proudly. "In fact, tomorrow he's bringing in other teachers to observe my technique."

Jake, I mean, Mr. Dirksen squinted angrily at me. Then, without a word, he turned and marched away.

Maybe I should have been happy, but I was really depressed. I'd turned Mr. Dirksen into a great teacher, but I was still Mr. Dirksen.

And that was the last thing in the world I wanted to be.

12

The next morning was Friday. I was coming to the end of my first week as Mr. Dirksen. I missed my home. I sort of missed my parents. I even missed my super perfect sister a little.

The doorbell rang. I knew it was Ms. Rogers. I went to the door and opened it.

"Good morning, Phil," she said, biting her lip nervously. Instead of the slacks and sweater she usually wore, this morning she was wearing a pretty pink dress. She'd also curled her hair and put on makeup.

"Good morning, Ms. Rogers, er, I mean, Kim," I said. "You look really pretty this morning."

"Why, thank you, Phil." Ms. Rogers blushed.

"So, would you like to come in?"

"No," Ms. Rogers said. "This morning I have a surprise for you. I'm taking you out for breakfast. We're going to celebrate."

"Oh, yeah? What's the occasion?" I asked.

Ms. Rogers looked surprised. "You don't know?"

I shook my head.

Ms. Rogers smiled. "Oh, you're just being modest. Alan must have told you that teachers will be coming in all day to observe how you teach class. You know very well that you've been chosen model teacher of the month."

"Model teacher of the month?" I couldn't believe it.

"Now come on, Mr. Modest," Ms. Rogers said, slipping her arm through mine. "We have to be quick or we'll be late for school."

We went to a restaurant a few blocks from school. Ms. Rogers kept giggling and blushing. I couldn't quite figure out what was going on, but I knew she was acting different.

I ordered pancakes, hashed browns, and sausage for breakfast. Ms. Rogers ordered a cup of tea and hardly touched it. She became very quiet, and a couple of times I looked up from my food and found her gazing dreamily at me.

Finally, I finished breakfast. "That was great. Thanks." I reached for my water glass to rinse the last bite down.

"You're welcome, Phil." Ms. Rogers took a sip of tea, then ran her fingertip around the rim of the tea cup. Suddenly she looked up and straight at me with her big blue eyes.

"Phil," she said. "I've been thinking about

something all week and I've finally gotten up the nerve to talk about it."

"Uh, okay," I said a little nervously.

"Now, I know this will seem very forward of me, but have you ever thought about marriage?"

"Ugh . . ." I was just in the middle of swallowing a big gulp of water. Suddenly I began to choke.

"Phil!" Ms. Rogers jumped up and slapped me on the back. Finally I swallowed.

"Are you all right?" she asked, looking very concerned.

"Uh, yeah, I think so," I gasped.

Ms. Rogers sat down again and looked straight at me. "What do you think?"

What did I think? I couldn't believe I'd even heard her correctly. "Did you say *marriage*?"

The corners of her pretty mouth turned down, and she looked sad. "I didn't think you'd react so negatively," she said with a sniff.

"To *marriage*?" My voice cracked a little. Ms. Rogers looked as if she was going to start crying right there in the middle of the restaurant. "Uh, no, no. Actually, I, er, I think about it all the time."

Ms. Rogers looked up surprised. "You do?"

"Uh, sure," I said. "It's just that it's not something I talk a lot about, you know?"

"Well, I'm going to make a confession," Ms. Rogers said. She began to twist her napkin nervously in her hand. "And I hope you won't laugh,

85

but I've had a crush on you ever since you dated my big sister, Ellen."

As Ms. Rogers said this, she slid her hand over mine.

"You have?" I swallowed.

Ms. Rogers nodded, never taking her eyes off me. "Of course, I never said anything because of Ellen. But now that she's become a nun, I felt I could take a chance. You're not angry, are you?"

"Uh, no, of course not," I said. "I, er, I think you're a wonderful person and really pretty. Uh, it's just that I'm not sure I'm ready . . ."

Ms. Rogers's forehead furrowed, and the corners of her mouth turned down again. She slid her hand off mine.

"I mean," I quickly added, "Not ready *today* . . . uh, I'm just not feeling like myself. But I'm sure that by tomorrow . . ." I trailed off, not certain what to say.

"What, Phil?" Ms. Rogers asked.

"Well, by tomorrow, it's just possible that I may feel like a whole different person," I said.

Ms. Rogers scowled. "I feel as if you're not being serious, Phil. I wish you understood how important this is to me. Over this past week, eating breakfast with you every morning, seeing how you've changed . . . I . . . I feel like I've fallen in love with you."

"Love?" The word croaked out of my, I mean, Mr. Dirksen's throat.

Ms. Rogers looked like she was going to cry again. "Is that so bad, Phil? Please don't tell me I've made a terrible mistake."

"Uh, no, no, of course you haven't," I said. "I . . . it's just that you've taken me by surprise."

"You haven't sensed it?" Ms. Rogers asked.

"Uh, well, maybe I have," I said, sliding my hand over hers and scrambling for excuses. "It's just that, well, the only time I get to see you is over breakfast, and I'm usually still not completely awake."

Ms. Rogers blinked. "You're right. I never thought about that."

I felt a moment of relief. It looked like I'd gotten out of *that* one.

Then Ms. Rogers leaned forward and squeezed my hand. "Oh, Phil, please come to my house tonight for dinner. We'll eat by candlelight. It will be so romantic. Please say you'll come?"

"A romantic dinner?" I swallowed hard.

"Oh, no, look at the time!" Ms. Rogers stared at her watch. "We're going to be late!"

We both jumped up from the table. Ms. Rogers rushed to pay the check, and I met her by the front door. We ran out to the car and drove quickly to school. As we entered the parking lot, I could see that the bell must have just rung because the kids were starting to go in.

Ms. Rogers quickly parked her car and turned toward me.

"Well, uh, thanks for breakfast," I said.

"You're welcome, Phil," she said. "And please promise me you'll keep this a secret. I just can't bear the thought of rumors about us spreading around school."

"I won't tell a soul, Kim," I said.

The next thing I knew, Ms. Rogers leaned over and kissed me on the lips.

"Come to dinner tonight, Phil," she whispered hotly. "I'll pick you up at six. I promise you won't regret it."

13

As soon as Jessica got into homeroom, I grabbed her and pulled her into a corner.

"We have a major problem!" I hissed.

"What?" Jessica asked.

"Ms. Rogers wants to marry me!"

"*What!?*" Jessica gasped too loudly.

"Shhh." I pressed Mr. Dirksen's finger against his lips. "It's top secret. She just took me out to breakfast. She basically told me she loves me and she wants me to come to a *very romantic* dinner at her house tonight."

"Oooh-la-la!" Jessica winked.

"It's not funny!" I whispered hoarsely. "What am I gonna do?"

"Go, of course."

"Are you crazy? She already kissed me in her car. What if she wants to do it some more?"

"Sounds great to me," Jessica said.

"Well, forget it," I said. "There are a lot of

things I'll do as Mr. Dirksen, but kissing other teachers isn't one of them."

"Then tell her you're busy."

"I can't."

"Why not?"

"Because I like Ms. Rogers. I'd really hate to hurt her feelings."

"Listen, you can either go or not go," Jessica said. "There aren't a lot of other choices."

I knew she was right. But I had to think of something.

Next period were the gifted and talented kids. The day before, a couple of them had stayed after class to ask me questions about the experiment we'd done. I'd sort of fudged the answers, but I could see they were starting to suspect something wasn't right. Today I faked having laryngitis, but I had a feeling I couldn't fool them much longer.

After that came study hall. I planned to use the study hall to come up with a way to get out of dinner with Ms. Rogers without hurting her feelings. Suddenly there was a knock on the classroom door. I looked up and saw Jake waving to me through the window.

"Uh, I'll be back in a second," I told the study hall, and then went out into the corridor.

Jake, I mean, Mr. Dirksen was standing out there with his arms crossed, looking upset. "You never told me I was supposed to go away camping with Josh and Andy tonight."

"I didn't think it mattered," I said with a shrug.

"Are you serious?" Jake, I mean, Mr. Dirksen sputtered. "You expect me to spend two days and two nights in a cabin in the woods with those hoodlums?"

"I don't expect you to do anything," I said.

But Mr. Dirksen hardly heard me. He was too busy ranting. "And what is with your sister? Do you know what she did to me last night? She beat me in backgammon, pinochle, and chess! Those are my best games!"

Way to go, Jessica! I couldn't help smiling.

"It's not funny," Jake, I mean, Mr. Dirksen snapped. "She's driving me crazy. The only thing worse would be spending the weekend with Josh and Andy."

"So what do you want to do?" I asked.

Jake, I mean, Mr. Dirksen looked pretty annoyed. "Well, how's your week been?"

"Oh, pretty good," I said. "I got you elected model teacher of the month."

"So I noticed."

"Oh, and you know Ms. Rogers?" I said.

"Of course I know Ms. Rogers."

"Well, remember all those years you were dating her big sister, Ellen?" I asked.

Jake, I mean, Mr. Dirksen narrowed his eyes. "What about them?"

91

"Well, it turns out that all that time Ms. Rogers had a big crush on you."

Jake's, I mean, Mr. Dirksen's jaw dropped. "She told you that?"

"We've had a lot of really nice talks this week. In fact, she's invited me to her house tonight for a very romantic dinner."

Jake, I mean, Mr. Dirksen stared at me.

"She wants to talk about marriage," I said.

"Ohmygod!" Jake, I mean, Mr. Dirksen gasped.

I couldn't help smiling. "That's usually my line, Mr. Dirksen."

Jake, I mean, Mr. Dirksen just stared back at me. "I think the time has come to switch back."

"Great!" I said with a big smile. "I knew you'd come around. What do you say we go to your house right after school and make the switch? Then you can go to Ms. Rogers' house for dinner, and I can go camping with my friends."

Jake, I mean, Mr. Dirksen didn't look very excited. "I wish it were that simple, Jake."

14

W hat are you talking about?" I asked. "All we
have to do is go to your house, get back into
the experiment and switch bodies again."

"No," Jake said. "We need a massive surge of
electricity. The sort of surge a bolt of lightning
might produce."

"You mean, we have to wait for another storm?"

"Not only for another storm. We have to wait
for another storm in which lightning strikes my
house."

"Well, what are the chances of something like
that happening?" I asked.

"Between now and six o'clock?" Jake glanced
out the window and shook my head. Outside, the
sky was blue. I remembered hearing a weather
forecast on the radio in Ms. Rogers's car saying
it would be clear and sunny all weekend.

"Well, what are we gonna do?" I asked.

"I don't know," Mr. Dirksen said, scratching
my head.

"But we'll have to come up with something," I pleaded.

Jake, I mean, Mr. Dirksen just shrugged his shoulders. "I don't know what to tell you, Jake."

I went back into study hall feeling terrible. We had to switch back to our normal bodies before six o'clock, or I was going to be in big trouble.

Teachers came and observed my classes all morning. I did the best job I could, but my mind was on other things. Finally, sixth-grade lunch came along. I knew Jessica had a study hall that period and I went and got her, telling the study hall teacher I needed her for a special project.

As we walked down the hallway I explained the problem we were facing.

"Where are we going?" Jessica asked.

"To the cafeteria. We're gonna find Jake, I mean, Mr. Dirksen and try to figure out a way to get the electricity we need."

We found him sitting alone at a table in the cafeteria, eating lunch and reading a book on electronics. Jessica and I sat down with him.

"You know, I really wish you wouldn't read stuff like that in public," I whispered. "People are gonna think I'm weird."

"Well, I wish your mother would think of something else to put in your lunch besides peanut butter and jelly sandwiches," he whispered back. "This is the fourth day in a row."

"I happen to *like* peanut butter and jelly," I said.

"Hey, cut it out," Jessica whispered. "This isn't helping things."

"Okay, look," I said. "Here's what I think. If we can't bring electricity to your experiment, then we're gonna have to take your experiment to where's there's electricity."

"Impossible," said Jake, I mean, Mr. Dirksen. "It would take a week to dismantle and reassemble my experiment."

"Isn't there any way to get enough electricity?" Jessica asked.

"It's practically impossible," Jake, I mean, Mr. Dirksen said. "I've estimated that the amount of electricity necessary to replicate the experiment would be in excess of one hundred times normal household electrical current."

"So it's not something you're going to find in your house," Jessica said. "Is there any place else nearby that would have that much electrical current?"

Mr. Dirksen thought for a moment. Then suddenly he snapped my fingers. "Yes! The electrical towers that run through the field behind my house. If there was some way to tap one of those lines, that would probably provide enough electricity."

"Great!" I said.

"The problem is, how do we get it?" Jake, I mean, Mr. Dirksen asked. "The towers are well over seventy feet tall. Even at their lowest points the lines must still be at least fifty feet off the ground."

We were all so involved in the problem that none of us noticed that Ms. Rogers, who was on lunch duty as usual, had come over.

"Having a conference?" she asked.

We all must have looked surprised. I tried to smile, and Ms. Rogers smiled back at me. Then she rubbed Jake on the head. "And how's my favorite troublemaker today?"

"Fine, Ms. Rogers, I mean, Kim," I said.

Ms. Rogers looked puzzled that I, I mean, Mr. Dirksen had answered instead of Jake.

"Me, too," Mr. Dirksen said with my mouth.

"Me, three," said Jessica.

"Well, I'm glad," Ms. Rogers said. Then she bent down and whispered quickly in my ear, "I hope you're looking forward to dinner as much as I am."

I straightened up and quickly nodded.

"Good, see you then." Ms. Rogers waved and walked away.

I glanced nervously at my former self. "So, uh, how do you feel about marriage?"

He just rolled his eyes.

"Okay, where were we?" Jessica asked. "Oh,

yeah, we have to find a way to get the power from the power lines down to Mr. Dirksen's house."

"Maybe we could climb up one of the towers," I said.

Jake, I mean, Mr. Dirksen shook his head. "No. Too dangerous. I can't allow it."

We kept puzzling over the problem. Then I glanced out the window toward the playground. Andy walked by, carrying something red.

"I've got it!" I cried and jumped up.

I ran outside to the playground. Andy was down at one end with his kite. He'd patched up the nose and broken wing with tape and sticks. He was just about to start running with it.

"Andy, wait!" I yelled and jogged toward him. Andy saw me coming and scowled.

"Uh, hi, Mr. Dirksen," he said. "What's up?"

"Did you build this magnificent kite all by yourself?" I asked.

"Uh, yeah, why?"

"I just think it's an incredible achievement," I said.

Andy looked at me funny. "You do?"

"Absolutely," I said. "Tell you what. How would you like an A this semester?"

"An *A*?"

"That's right," I said.

"Wow, sure," Andy grinned. "I never got one of those."

"Okay, here's the deal," I said. "I'll trade you an A for your kite."

Andy glanced down at his battered kite and then gave me a skeptical look. "Is this a trick?"

"No, Andy," I said. "I give you my word. Your kite for an A."

"Okay, Mr. Dirksen, sure." Andy handed me his kite.

"Thanks, Andy," I said and ran back toward the cafeteria.

"How'd you get that?" Jake, I mean, Mr. Dirksen asked when I returned with Andy's kite.

"Easy, I traded Andy an A for it," I said.

Jake's jaw dropped. "You promised Andy Kent an A?"

"No," I said with a smile. "*You* did."

After school, Jessica, Mr. Dirksen, and I met at his house.

"I've been thinking it over," Jake, I mean, Mr. Dirksen said. "We'll use my ultra-light, super-conductive high-voltage wire as string for the kite. We'll sail the kite over the power line, then run it down to my experiment."

Jake, I mean, Mr. Dirksen went into the garage and got the spool of wire. He tied it to the kite, and then we all went out to the field behind his house.

I noticed that Jake, I mean, Mr. Dirksen was carrying a pair of heavy rubber gloves.

"I know that we have to do this in order to switch back to our regular bodies," he said. "But I feel it is my duty as an adult to warn you that what we are about to do is extremely dangerous and you must never attempt something like this on your own."

Jessica and I glanced at each other.

"Uh, it's not like I have a regular need for a million volts of electricity," I said.

Jake, I mean, Mr. Dirksen stopped and stared at me. "That's a good point, Jake."

The field was covered with tall grass and wild flowers. We walked to a place between two towers where the power lines dipped to their lowest point. They still seemed really high in the air. Jake, I mean, Mr. Dirksen tied the wire to the kite and then slipped on the heavy rubber gloves.

"I hope this works," he said nervously.

"Listen," I said. "Maybe I ought to do this."

"No." Jake, I mean, Mr. Dirksen shook his head. "It's too dangerous."

"Yeah, but if you mess up, I could get killed," I said.

"So could I," said Jake, I mean, Mr. Dirksen.

The two of us stared at each other uncertainly.

"Look," Jessica said. "It really doesn't matter which of you does it as long as *one* of you does. And you better hurry or you're going to run out of time."

Jake, I mean, Mr. Dirksen took the kite and walked way down the field.

"Boy, I hope this works," I said.

"*You* hope it works," said Jessica. "If it doesn't, I don't know what I'll do. Last night he not only did the dishes and swept the kitchen floor, he actually vacuumed the living room. He's making me look really bad."

Across the field, Jake, I mean, Mr. Dirksen started to run. Jessica and I crossed our fingers.

"Look, it's going up!" Jessica cried. She was right. The kite began to climb into the air toward the power lines. Jake, I mean, Mr. Dirksen ran like crazy under it. The kite kept climbing up.

My sister and I held our breaths.

"I think it's going to work!" Jessica cried.

The kite climbed higher and higher. In a few moments it would cross the power lines!

Suddenly it stopped climbing.

For a moment it just hung in the sky. Jake, I mean, Mr. Dirksen stopped running and stared up at it.

The kite turned and started to plunge down like a dive-bomber . . . straight for him!

"Aaaahhhh!" He screamed and disappeared into the tall grass.

15

Jessica and I ran toward the spot where he'd disappeared.

"Jake!" she shouted. "Are you okay?"

"Mr. Dirksen!" I shouted. "Where are you?"

"Here," a weak voice gasped.

Jessica and I ran to the spot where the voice had come from. Jake, I mean, Mr. Dirksen was lying in the grass. The kite had crashed to the ground a few feet away.

"It almost killed me," he whimpered as Jessica and I helped him to his feet.

"I forgot to tell you. It's a kamikaze kite," I said.

"What?"

"It tries to kill whoever flies it."

"Well, it did a pretty good job of killing itself," Jake, I mean, Mr. Dirksen said. He was right. The nose had been crushed again and this time both wings were broken.

"Can we fix it?" Jessica asked.

Jake, I mean, Mr. Dirksen shook his head. "It appears to be damaged beyond repair. And even if we did fix it, it might try to kill whoever flew it again."

For a few moments we stood in the field without talking. It seemed like we'd hit a dead end. There was no way to get the electricity we needed to switch back.

"I can't believe I'm gonna be stuck in this body for the rest of my life!" I groaned.

"It's not *that* bad," Jake, I mean, Mr. Dirksen said.

"That's easy for *you* to say," I sniffed. "You didn't get robbed of twenty-three years of your life. You'll get to be a teenager twice!"

"I hated being a teenager," Jake, I mean, Mr. Dirksen muttered.

"Figures," I said. It was hard to believe that anybody could hate being a teenager. But if anyone could, it had to be Mr. Dirksen.

"What do you mean, it figures?" Jake, I mean, Mr. Dirksen huffed.

"Will you two please stop it!" Jessica snapped. "Now there has to be a way to get that wire up to those power lines."

"Maybe we could build a rocket," I said. "We could go back to school and mix up some gunpowder and make a rocket."

"There isn't time," Jessica said. "Ms. Rogers is

supposed to pick up Mr. Dirksen in an hour. And you're supposed to leave on your camping trip in an hour and a half."

I stared up at the lines. What could get high enough, if not a kite or a rocket?

A baseball . . .

"I've got it!" I said. "We'll get a baseball and tape the wire to it. Then we'll throw the baseball over the electric lines."

Jessica stared up at the lines and back at me.

"It's pretty high," she said. "But it's worth a try."

I remembered the baseball in Mr. Dirksen's closet at home. We taped one end of the ultra-thin wire to it and went back out to the field. Since it was my idea, I tried to throw the ball first. It didn't come anywhere close to going over the lines.

"What a wimpy arm you have," I told Jake, I mean, Mr. Dirksen.

"Don't knock it," he said. "Right now that's your arm and it may stay that way for a long time to come."

"Here, let me try," Jessica said. She took the ball and heaved it toward the lines. It came a lot closer than my throw had, but it was still short.

Jessica tried again.

And again.

And again . . .

But she couldn't get the ball over the power lines either.

"Forget it." She shook her head sadly. "It's no use."

The three of us stood in the tall grass. As the implications of what lay ahead sank in, I grew really depressed.

"I can't believe it," I moaned, looking at Mr. Dirksen. "I just can't believe I'm gonna be you for the rest of my life."

"Listen, being you is no picnic, either," Jake, I mean, Mr. Dirksen replied. "And I was a lot happier without a big sister."

"Drop dead." Jessica glared at him. Then she turned to me. "Come on, Jake, let's go. You may look like a dorky science teacher, but inside I know you're still my little brother."

We started to walk away through the tall grass. It was time to start preparing for a new life. I had to start figuring out what to do about Ms. Rogers, and whether or not I still wanted to be a nerdy science teacher.

"Hey!" Jake, I mean, Mr. Dirksen yelled behind us.

Jessica and I turned. Jake, I mean, Mr. Dirksen picked up the baseball.

"You didn't give me a chance," he said.

Jessica and I looked at each other. "This should be good," Jessica said with a smirk.

"Hey, maybe he can do it," I said.

"Not a chance," Jessica said.

I watched myself wind up and throw. The ball sailed up into the air, but fell short.

"Come on, let's go home," Jessica said.

"No, wait," I said.

I watched as I, I mean Mr. Dirksen picked up the ball again. *Come on*, I thought. *You can do it!*

I, I mean, Mr. Dirksen heaved the ball again.

And again it fell short.

"This is dumb," Jessica said.

A dozen yards away, I, I mean, Mr. Dirksen picked up the ball again. Except this time, instead of trying to throw it, he just stared at me.

I stared back into my own eyes. "If you do it, I'll be a model student for the rest of my life," I yelled.

"Promise?" Jake, I mean, Mr. Dirksen asked.

"I swear it," I yelled.

I watched as I went into a wind up . . . and heaved with all my might.

The ball sailed up and up. It went higher than the other throws . . .

Higher even than the best my sister could do . . .

It just cleared the power line!

A spark crackled as the ultra-fine wire fell over the line.

"I did it!" Jake, I mean, Mr. Dirksen and I shouted at the same time.

We stared at each other.

"You didn't do it!" he yelled. "*I* did!"

"No, *I* did!" I yelled back.

"You *both* did!" Jessica shouted at us. "Now come on, we don't have much time!"

16

Jake, I mean, Mr. Dirksen pulled on the heavy rubber gloves and picked up the spool of wire. We quickly jogged back toward his house, letting the wire spool out behind us. When we got back to his garage, he screwed the wire into a big switch on the wall. Other wires led from the switch to the experiment.

"All right, Jake," he said. "You sure you're ready?"

"You bet."

"Stand next to the cage, as close as you can get," Jake, I mean, Mr. Dirksen said, stepping over to the computer console and typing something. Then he looked over at my sister. "Jessica, throw the switch when I tell you to."

I stood by the cage. Jessica stood by the switch. Jake, I mean, Mr. Dirksen stepped toward his cage, but then stopped. He put his hands on his hips and bent backward.

"Ahh!" he sighed. "I just want to remember what it feels like to have a good back."

"So do I," I said.

Jake, I mean, Mr. Dirksen smirked. "Don't forget, you promised to be the best-behaved student in my class."

"Yeah, yeah, okay." He didn't have to remind me.

Jake, I mean, Mr. Dirksen stepped near the other cage and turned toward my sister. "Throw the switch, Jessica."

There was a bright flash and a loud buzzing sound. I felt the hair rise on Mr. Dirksen's arms and a force surged through me.

"All right!" I shouted, thrusting my fist into the air triumphantly. "We did it!" I was so happy I even jumped off the ground. But when I landed, a spasm of pain shot through my back.

"Ouch! What the . . . ?" I was still in Mr. Dirksen's body! I looked across the garage and saw the weirdest thing. It was Jake, but he was bald!

"Wow, Mr. Dirksen," Jessica said, looking up at me. "You look good with hair."

"I do?" I felt my head. I had hair! Suddenly I realized what had happened. "Wait a minute! This isn't Mr. Dirksen's hair. It's *my* hair! And I want it back on *my* head."

"You mean it didn't work?" Jessica gasped.

"No way," I said. "I'm still Jake inside

Mr. Dirksen. Only now I've got Jake's hair. What went wrong?"

"I don't know," Mr. Dirksen in my bald-headed body replied. "According to my calculations you should be Jake and I should be me . . . with hair."

"It was a trick!" I gasped. "you tried to steal my hair!"

"Not steal it, Jake. I just wanted to borrow some."

"No deal," I said. "I want my hair back. *All* of it."

"I'm not sure it's possible," said Mr. Dirksen.

"Oh, yeah? Then you better plan on being a bald teenager for the next eight years," I said. "Because I'm not switching back until Jake has his hair again."

"Come on, Jake," said Mr. Dirksen in my bald-headed body. "They're doing marvelous things with hair transplants these days."

"Forget it," I said. "I can't believe you tried to steal my hair."

"Oh, all right." Mr. Dirksen, in my bald-headed body, went over to a computer console and typed something on the keyboard.

"You promise no more tricks?" I asked.

"I promise," Jake, I mean, Mr. Dirksen sighed as he walked back to his cage. "Okay, Jessica, throw the switch again."

There was another bright flash and more buzzing. Once again I felt a force surge through me. Then everything went black.

"Jake?" I heard a faint voice. It sounded like it was coming from far away.

"Jake, are you okay?" The voice came closer. I opened my eyes and looked up into Jessica's face.

Everything looked fuzzy.

"I need my glasses," I groaned, feeling around on the garage floor.

"No, you don't," Jessica said.

"Yeah, I do. I can't see anything without them."

"Jake, you've never worn glasses," Jessica said.

Suddenly I understood. I reached up and felt my head. *I had hair!*

I had my old body back! I jumped up and bent backward. My back didn't hurt!

"Ow!" Across the garage, Mr. Dirksen was also bending back. But *his* back did hurt.

"I'm already starting to regret this," he groaned.

"Listen, Mr. Dirksen, you've got to get ready for dinner with Ms. Rogers," Jessica said.

"You're right," Mr. Dirksen gasped. "I must go change my clothes."

He started toward the door. Jessica and I glanced at each other. Then we both shouted, *"Wait!"*

"What?" Mr. Dirksen asked.

"Don't change into those dumb old brown clothes," I said.

"Why not?" Mr. Dirksen asked.

"Because that's the old you," Jessica explained. "Ms. Rogers loves the *new* you."

"The one who wears jeans and denim shirts and does science experiments," I said.

"But . . . that's not me," Mr. Dirksen stammered.

"Look," I said, growing impatient, "Ms. Rogers is a really sweet, really pretty, really nice person. Do you want to marry her or not?"

"Well . . ." Mr. Dirksen rubbed his chin. "I always did like her more than Ellen. Of course, I met Ellen first and, being a gentleman, there was nothing I could do about it."

Jessica and I glanced at each other.

"Ellen became a nun," Jessica said. "I'm sure she won't mind."

"I suppose you're right," Mr. Dirksen said, rubbing his hairless chin. "And it would be nice to have some female companionship."

"Does that mean yes?" I asked.

"Well, I'd say I'd be inclined to marry Kim," Mr. Dirksen said with a nod. But then he frowned and shook his head. "No, it won't work."

"Why not?" Jessica asked.

"Because she's not really in love with *me*," Mr. Dirksen said.

"Yes, she is," I said. "All you have to do is stop wearing those dorky clothes and loosen up a little. I mean, I'm not a science teacher, but I managed to do a pretty decent job for a week. And you can be the person Ms. Rogers loves."

Mr. Dirksen thought it over for a moment. "Can I at least grow my beard back?"

Jessica and I glanced at each other again.

"No," we both said.

"At least, not until *after* you're married," Jessica added.

"Oh, all right." Mr. Dirksen turned toward the door, then stopped again. "Jake?"

"Yeah?"

"I suppose I owe you some thanks," Mr. Dirksen said. "You showed me how to be a better teacher, and you got Kim to fall in love with me."

"No problem, Mr. Dirksen," I said. Then Jessica nudged me. I knew what she was thinking. "I guess I owe you some thanks, too," I said.

"Oh?" Mr. Dirksen's eyebrows went up.

"Now I know how things look from the other side," I said.

Mr. Dirksen scowled, then smiled as if he understood. I smiled back. I had a feeling Mr. Dirksen and I would get along better from now on.

Moments later, Jessica and I started walking back toward our house.

"Are you *really* going to start behaving in his class?" she asked.

"I guess," I said. "I mean, it seems like a pretty awesome task, but maybe if he really makes it interesting, I could do it."

"Well, I've decided that from now on I won't try to be better than you at everything," Jessica said. "Especially if you promise you won't straighten the dishes in the kitchen cabinets without being asked."

"That wasn't me," I said. "That was Mr. Dirksen."

"I know," Jessica said. "I'm just afraid that a little might have rubbed off."

Epilogue

I made it home in time to pack and go on the camping trip. Josh and Andy acted a little weird at first, but as soon as we got to the cabin, I shook up a can of soda and sprayed them with it. Pretty soon things were back to normal.

And I did start to behave in Mr. Dirksen's class. It wasn't *that* hard. Mr. Dirksen actually let us do some experiments so that class wasn't so boring. The weird thing is, I've started to behave in most of my other classes, too. I'm not sure why. I guess maybe I really do see things from the other side now.

Life is pretty much back to normal at home. I help out a little more than I used to. But not too much, because I don't want to make Jessica look bad or anything. And she actually let me win a game of "Horse" in the driveway the other day.

Oh, yeah, I almost forgot. About a month after Mr. Dirksen and I switched back, I was sitting in the cafeteria with Josh and Andy when Ms. Rogers came over.

"How's my favorite ex-troublemaker?" she asked and rubbed my head with her hand.

"Ow!" I said, feeling something hard scrape my scalp.

"Oops, sorry, Jake, I keep forgetting I have this ring." Ms. Rogers showed me a small diamond ring on her ring finger.

"So you and Mr. Dirksen are getting married, huh?" I said.

Ms. Rogers nodded and blushed a little. They'd managed to keep it a secret for a couple of weeks, but then the word slowly got out and now the whole school knew.

"Think I made the right choice?" Ms. Rogers asked.

"Oh, sure, Ms. Rogers," I said. "He's a great guy. You couldn't have done better if I'd married you myself."

"Well, that's sweet," Ms. Rogers said. "But I think you'd be a little too young."

"Oh, you never know, Ms. Rogers," I said with a wink. "You never know."

About the Author

Todd Strasser is an award-winning author of many novels for young readers. Among his best known are *The Mall from Outer Space* and *The Diving Bell*. He also wrote Scholastic's novelizations of *Home Alone*™ and *Home Alone 2*™.

In addition to writing, Todd Strasser frequently visits schools, where he speaks about writing and conducts writing workshops. He lives with his wife and children in New York State.

APPLE®PAPERBACKS

Pick an Apple and Polish Off Some Great Reading!

BEST-SELLING APPLE TITLES

- ❏ MT43944-8 **Afternoon of the Elves** Janet Taylor Lisle **$2.99**
- ❏ MT41624-3 **The Captive** Joyce Hansen **$3.50**
- ❏ MT43266-4 **Circle of Gold** Candy Dawson Boyd **$3.50**
- ❏ MT44064-0 **Class President** Johanna Hurwitz **$2.75**
- ❏ MT45436-6 **Cousins** Virginia Hamilton **$2.95**
- ❏ MT43130-7 **The Forgotten Door** Alexander Key **$2.95**
- ❏ MT44569-3 **Freedom Crossing** Margaret Goff Clark **$2.95**
- ❏ MT44036-5 **George Washington's Socks**
  Elvira Woodruff **$2.95**
- ❏ MT41708-8 **The Secret of NIMH** Robert C. O'Brien **$2.75**
- ❏ MT42537-4 **Snow Treasure** Marie McSwigan **$2.95**
- ❏ MT46921-5 **Steal Away** Jennifer Armstrong **$3.50**

Available wherever you buy books, or use this order form.

- -

SCHOLASTIC INC.
Box 7502, 2931 East McCarty Street, Jefferson City, MO 65102

Please send me the books I have checked above. I am enclosing $ _____ (please add $2.00 to cover shipping and handling). Send check or money order—no cash or C.O.D.s please.

Name_____ Birth Date_____

Address_____

City_____ State/Zip_____

Please allow four to six weeks for delivery. Offer good in the U.S.A. only. Sorry, mail orders are not available to residents of Canada. Prices subject to change.